Valerie Martin is the author of two collections of short fiction and six novels, including *Italian Fever*, *The Great Divorce*, and *Mary Reilly*. Her most recent book is a non-fiction work on St Francis of Assisi: *Salvation: Scenes from the Life of St Francis*. She resides in upstate New York.

Also by Valerie Martin

Property

~

Valerie
Martin

ABACUS

An *Abacus* Book

First published in Great Britain as a
paperback original in 2003 by Abacus

Published by arrangement with Doubleday, a division of
The Doubleday Broadway Publishing Group,
a division of Random House, Inc.

Copyright © Valerie Martin 2003

The moral right of the author has been asserted.

A CIP catalogue record for this book
is available from the British Library.

ISBN 0 349 11583 4

Typeset by Palimpsest Book Production Limited,
Polmont, Stirlingshire
Printed and bound in Great Britain by
Clays Ltd, St Ives Plc.

Abacus
An imprint of
Time Warner Books UK
Brettenham House
Lancaster Place
London WC2E 7EN

www.TimeWarnerBooks.co.uk

What social virtues are possible in a society of which injustice is the primary characteristic?

—Harriet Martineau,
Society in America, 1837

Amount Brot Forward   608.75

17. One Negro girl named Isabel aged fifteen years
a Slave for life. adjudged to Philip Richards for the sum
of Eight Hundred fifty dollars. Ursin Hebert security   850.00

    Ursin + Hebert   Philip + Richard

18. One Negro woman named Celeste aged twenty five years.
a Slave for life. adjudged to Francois Marceau for the
Sum of Eight Hundred dollars.   Marceau   800.00

Wit. Berard

19. One Negro girl named Rosy aged ten years a Slave for life
adjudged to Francois Marceau for the Sum of Six Hundred
and Twelve dollars.   Marceau   612.00

Wit. Berard

20. One negro man named Michel aged twenty years a Slave for life
adjudged to Jacques Fortin jun. for the Sum of Eleven Hundred and
Fifty dollars. Dame Julie Hebert security.   1150.00

       ×   Jacques Fortin

21. One Negro Boy named Louis aged thirteen years a Slave for life adjudged
to. Dame Marie Angele Fortin. wife of Francois Cadmus. authorised
by the Judge. for the sum of Seven Hundred & fifty five dollars   755.00

      Angele + Fortin

22. One certain tract of Land situated in the Parish of Lafayette containing
Four arpents front on the East Side of the River Vermillion with the
depth of Forty two arpents. together with all & singular the houses,
magazines, fencing & &c of every description, it being the late residence of said deceased & bounded above & below by the Lands of Thomas
Berard, also one other Small tract of Land lying being & situated
in the Parish aforesaid containing One arpent front with the depth
of Forty One arpents. more or less & fronting on the west bank of the river
Vermillion & bounded above by the Lands of Dame Julie Hebert widow of
Jacques Fortin & below by the lands of St Geuidry. adjudged. also
together to Thos Berard for the Sum of One Thousand & fifty dollars   1050

           5805.75

      Marceau   Thos Berard

PART ONE

~

Plantation Life
1828

It never ends. I watched him through the spyglass to see what the game would be. There were five of them. He gets them all gathered at the river's edge and they are nervous. If they haven't done this before, they've heard about it. First he reads to them from the Bible. I don't have to hear it to know what passage it is. Then they have to strip, which takes no time as they are wearing only linen pantaloons. One by one they must grasp the rope, swing over the water, and drop in. It's brutally hot; the cool water is a relief, so they make the best of it. He encourages them to shout and slap at one another once they are in the water. Then they have to come out and do it again, only this time they hang on the rope two at a time, which means one has to hold on to the other. They had gotten this far when I looked.

Two boys were pulling the rope, one holding on while the other clutched his shoulders. They were laughing because they were slippery. The sun made their bodies glisten and steam like a horse's flanks after a long run. The boy on the ground ran down the bank and off they went, out over the water, releasing the rope at the highest point of its arc and crashing into the smooth surface below like wounded black geese. He hardly watched them. He was choosing the next two, directing one to catch the rope on its return, running his hands over the shoulders of the other, which made the boy cower and study the ground. I couldn't watch anymore.

They have to keep doing this, their lithe young bodies displayed to him in various positions. When he gets them up to three or four at a time, he watches closely. The boys rub against each other; they can't help it. Their limbs become entwined, they struggle to hang on, and it isn't long before one comes out of the water with his member raised. That's what the game is for. This boy tries to stay in the water, he hangs his head as he comes out, thinking every thought he can to make the tumescence subside. This is what proves they are brutes, he says, and have not the power of reason. A white man, knowing he would be beaten for it, would not be able to raise his member.

He has his stick there by the tree; it is never far from him. The boys fall silent as he takes it up. Sometimes the offending boy cries out or tries to run away, but he's no match for this grown man with his stick. The servant's tumescence subsides as quickly as the master's rises, and the latter will last until he gets to the quarter. If he can find the boy's mother, and she's pretty, she will pay dearly for rearing an unnatural child.

This is only one of his games. When he comes back to

the house he will be in a fine humor for the rest of the day.

Often, as I look through the glass, I hear in my head an incredulous refrain: *This is my husband, this is my husband.*

~

In the morning he was in a fury because Mr Sutter has gotten into such a standoff with one of the negroes that he has had him whipped and it will be a week before he can work again. They are cutting wood in shifts and there are no hands to spare, or so my husband has persuaded himself. The negro, Leo, is the strongest worker we have. He maintains Leo was never a problem until Sutter decided he was insolent. Sutter's real grievance, he says, is that Leo has befriended a woman Sutter wants for himself. I had to listen to all this at breakfast. He cursed and declared he would kill Sutter, then sent back the food, saying it was cold. Sarah went out with the plate. He leaned back in his chair and put his hand over his eyes. 'She's poisoning me,' he said.

When Sarah came back, he pretended to soften. 'Is Walter in the house?' he asked. 'Send him to me.'

So then we had the little bastard running up and down the dining room, putting his grubby fingers in the serving plates, eating bits of meat from his father's hand like a dog. Sarah leaned against the sideboard and watched, but she didn't appear to enjoy the sight much more than I did. The child is a mad creature, like a beautiful and vicious little wildcat. It wouldn't surprise me to see him clawing the portieres. He has his father's curly red hair and green eyes, his mother's golden skin, her full pouting lips. He speaks

5

a strange gibberish even Sarah doesn't understand. His father dotes on him for a few minutes now and then, but he soon tires of this and sends him away to the kitchen, where he lives under the table, torturing a puppy Delphine was fool enough to give him. Once the boy was gone, he turned his attention to Sarah. 'Go down and see to Leo,' he said. 'And give me a report in my office when you have done.'

She nodded, eyes cast down. Then he pushed back his chair and went out without speaking to me.

'He thinks you are poisoning him,' I said when he was gone, watching her face. Something flickered at the corner of her mouth; was it amusement? 'I'll have more coffee,' I said.

〜

On the pretense that she is of some use to me, I had Sarah in my room all morning with the baby she calls Nell, a dark, ugly thing, but quiet enough. He hates the sight of this one. It's too dark to be his, or so he thinks, though stranger things have happened, and everyone knows a drop of negro blood does sometimes overflow like an inkpot in the child of parents who are passing for white, to the horror of the couple and their other children as well. Somehow Sarah has prevailed upon my husband, with tears and cajoling, I've no doubt, to let her keep this baby in the house until it is weaned. At first she had it in the kitchen, but she was up and down the stairs a hundred times a day, which made him so irritable he demanded that I do something about it. I told Sarah to bring a crate from the quarter and put it in the corner of my room, which earned me one of her rare straightforward looks that I take to mean she's pleased.

It was so hot, I had her fan me. So there we sat, I with my eternal sewing, Sarah plying the fan, and the baby sleeping in her box. She has rigged the box out absurdly with a ticking mattress stuffed with moss and covered by a rag quilt. She even tacked a loop of willow across the middle to hold up a piece of mosquito net. 'Is she a princess?' I said when I saw this ridiculous contraption. 'If she not itchy, she won' cry,' Sarah replied. This, I had to admit, was a reasonable assertion. It is one of the annoying things about her; on those occasions when she bothers to speak, she makes sense.

After a while the baby whimpered. Sarah took it up to suckle, holding it in one arm and working the fan with the other. She had pulled her chair up behind mine so I couldn't watch this process, but I could hear the nuzzling, snuffling sound, mewing a little now and then like a kitten. I don't understand why she is so determined to suckle this one, as it will be passed down to the quarter as soon as it's weaned and sold away when it is old enough to work. He won't get much for her. Ugly, dark little girls aren't easy to sell. It would be a good joke on him if he had to give her away.

Eventually I grew bored and tried talking to her, a largely hopeless enterprise. 'You went down to tend to Leo?' I said.

'I did,' she replied.

'Is he bad?'

'He'll live.'

'Who did the whipping?'

'I don' know.'

So much for conversation.

At dinner he was gloomy. The new rollers for the sugar press have come. He spent the morning trying to get them installed and cut his hand badly in the process. It is all Sutter's fault because he couldn't use Leo, who has more experience with the press than anyone on the place. He had to call in two boys from the field who didn't know their right hands from their left and couldn't hold up their own pants. If Sutter wanted to whip boys near to death, he said, why couldn't he choose worthless ones like these two and not the only useful negro on the place.

When Sarah brought the potatoes in, he took a spoon from the bowl straight to his mouth and then spat it into his plate. 'Are we not possessed of a warming dish in this house!' he cried out. Sarah picked up the bowl, pulled the plate away, and headed for the door. He wiped his mouth vigorously with his napkin, swallowed half a glass of wine. 'I swear she puts them in the icehouse.'

I looked at him for a few moments blankly, without comment, as if he was speaking a foreign language. This unnerves him. It's a trick I learned from Sarah. 'Since there are no servants presently available, Mistress Manon,' he said, 'I'll have to prevail on you to serve me some meat.'

I got up, went to the sideboard, and served out a few slices of roast. When I set the plate in front of him, he

8

attacked it like a starving man. Sarah came back in carrying a bowl wrapped in a cloth which sent up a puff of steam when she opened it. He grunted approval as she spooned a portion onto his plate.

I went to my place but couldn't bring myself to sit down. 'I have a headache,' I said. 'I'll have dinner later in my room.' He nodded, then, as I was leaving, he said, 'I would like to speak to you in my office before supper.'

'Would four o'clock be convenient?' I said.

'Yes,' he replied through a mouthful of food.

~

He prides himself on being different from his neighbors, but his office looks exactly like every planter's office in the state: the good carpet, the leather-topped desk, the engravings of racehorses, the Bible with the ribbon marker that never moves, employed as a paperweight, the cabinet stocked with strong drink. I kept him waiting a quarter of an hour to irritate him. When I went in he was sitting at the desk poring over his account books. He does this by the hour, totaling up long lists of supplies and others of debt. Without looking at me, he observed, 'Someone is stealing corn.'

'Are you sure there's no mistake in your figures?' I asked.

He looked up. 'Will you sit down?' he said, gesturing to a chair. I was so surprised by his civil tone that I did as he asked, and busied myself arranging my skirts until he should be moved to reveal the motive of his summons.

'Three of Joel Borden's negroes ran away on Sunday,'

he began. 'Last night one of them broke into Duplantier's smokehouse. The houseboy saw him and raised the alarm, but they didn't catch him. Duplantier says he was carrying a pistol, though where he got it no one knows. Borden isn't missing any firearms.'

'I see,' I said.

'So they're coming this way.'

'Yes,' I agreed.

'They'll probably try to pass through the bottomland and get to the boat landing. I'm joining the patrol at dark. I've got two sentries I can trust here; they'll be moving around all night. I'll lock the house and put the dogs in the kitchen.'

'Delphine is afraid of the dogs.'

'Well, she'll just have to be afraid,' he said impatiently. 'She'll be a heap more scared if one of these bucks comes through the window with a pistol.'

'That's true,' I said.

'I want you and Sarah to stay in your room, lock the door, and don't come out for anything until I come back.'

I kept my eyes down. 'Wouldn't it be better for Sarah to stay in the kitchen with Delphine?'

'Don't worry about Delphine. She'll have Walter and Rose with her.'

Walter is a mad child and Rose a flighty girl. Neither would be of much use in a crisis. 'And Sarah will be safer with me,' I observed.

'You'll be safer together,' he corrected me, scowling at my impertinence, then neatly changing the subject. 'It's all Borden's fault. He doesn't half-feed his negroes and his overseer is the meanest man on earth. The ham they got from Duplantier was probably the first decent food they'd had in a year.'

'Is Joel here or in town?'

'He came up quick enough when he heard about it. Now he's grumbling that he'll be out two thousand dollars if we kill them. Not one man on the patrol is going to risk his life to save one of these damned runaways. If we can find them, they'll be better off dead than dragged back to Borden's overseer, and I've no doubt they know it.'

'Then they must be desperate.'

He gave me a long look, trying to detect any mockery in this remark. Evidently he found none and his inspection shifted from my mood to my person, where he found cause for a suspicion of extravagance. 'Is that a new dress?' he asked.

'No,' I replied. 'I retrimmed it with some lace Aunt Lelia sent.'

His eyes swept over my figure in that rapacious way I find so unsettling. 'You've changed the neck.'

He couldn't be dismissed as an unobservant man. 'Yes,' I said. 'The styles have changed.'

'I wonder how you know when you have so little society.'

'I copied it from a paper my aunt sent with the lace.'

'It's very becoming,' he said.

There was a time when I was moved by compliments, but that time is long behind us, as we both know. Still he manages to work up some feeling about what he imagines is my ingratitude. 'I'm sorry to vex you by remarking on your appearance, Manon,' he said. 'You are free to leave, if you've no business of your own to discuss with me.'

I stood up. What business might that be? I wondered. Perhaps he'd care to have a look at *my* accounts: on one side my grievances, on the other my resolutions, all in perfect balance. I allowed my eyes to rest upon his face. He brought his hand to his mustache, smoothing down one side of it, a nervous habit of his. It's always the right side, never the left. Looking at him makes my spine stiffen; I could feel the straightness of it, the elongation of my neck as I turned away. There was the rustling sound of my skirt sweeping against the carpet as I left the room, terminating thereby another lively interview with my husband.

~

My mother always slept with a servant in the room, a practice I disdain in my own house. I had Sarah bring up a pallet and put it next to her baby's box. At first I thought I would place the screen so that I wouldn't have to see her sleeping, then I decided to block off an area for the chamber pot, as I was even less inclined to witness her at that activity. 'I hope you don't snore,' I said, as she was struggling with the screen.

It was hot in the room and I was vexed by the stupid business, the unnecessary panic, the stamping and bellowing of the men who had already descended upon our dining room, where they were displaying their rifles to each other and gulping down his best whiskey. Their voices washed in under the door, droning and raucous by turns. There was much bandying about of Joel Borden's name. They consider him a fop and a dandy, too interested in the next gala party to attend to his own crops. He is in the city more than at his own house, and the result is that his negroes are loose in the countryside.

I bade Sarah brush my hair while I waited for them to leave. It relaxes me and gives her something to do. She was looking gloomy, no more pleased than I was to be shut up in close quarters. A fly buzzed around, landing on the mirror and crawling over our reflection. 'Kill it,' I said. She dropped my hair and took up a swatter. When she had smashed the thing, she wiped it away with a bit of rag. No sooner was this done than another came buzzing in at the window, skittering madly across the ceiling. 'Finish my hair,' I said, 'and then fill the trap.' She took up my hair, which was already damp with perspiration, and began braiding it. I looked at her reflection, her face intent on the task, a few drops of moisture on her forehead. She's an excellent hairdresser. I watched her long fingers smoothing back the waves at my temple; she watched her hands too, looking for any gray hairs to pull out. My hair is thick, wavy, too brassy, in my opinion, though Father always called it his golden treasure.

When she was done, she pinned the braid up and my neck was cool for the first time all day. We could hear the chairs scraping downstairs, the heavy footsteps and laughter as the men went out on the porch, then the shouting as they mounted their horses and clattered off on their mission. Behind that racket a dense stillness announced the long night ahead of us.

'Do you know anything about these runaways?' I asked

her. She was filling the base of the trap with sugar water.

'One of them is brother to Delphine,' she said. She looked up over the glass to see how this information affected me.

Were they coming this way in the hope of help from Delphine? I thought. What if she was foolish enough to let them into the house? But she wouldn't do that; she would be too afraid of the dogs. That was why my husband had closed them up with her and sent Sarah to hide with me. 'Did he tell you to stay with me?' I asked. 'Or was it your idea?'

For answer all I got was one of her smirks.

~

I was dreaming. There was a fox. As I approached the animal it opened its mouth as if panting and a high-pitched scream came out. I woke up inside that scream, which was in my room, a shriek so loud and harsh I thought a woman was being murdered outside my window. I remembered Delphine in the kitchen, the runaway negroes. I sat up, breathless, ready to leap from the bed, but before I did, the scream moved rapidly, past the house, swooping away in the direction of the cabins.

'An owl,' I said.

I heard a rustling sound in the corner of the room, which gave me another shock until I recalled that I was not alone. The moonlight made a bright swath across the floor, ending at Sarah's pallet. I made out the white contour of her shift and the light of her eyes watching me steadily. We looked

14

at each other without speaking while my heart slowed to a normal pace. Her baby made a muffled cry and she turned to take it up in her arms.

'Has he come back?' I asked.

''Bout an hour ago,' she said. 'You was asleep.'

I fell back on my pillow. There was a thin breeze pressing the net lightly toward me. I loosened the front of my shift to have advantage of it. When I turned on my side, I looked down to where Sarah lay, the child curled up at her side, her wide eyes watching me, and I thought, she has been watching me like that this entire night.

~

At breakfast he was ravenous. I ate a piece of bread with Creole cheese and drank a cup of strong coffee while I watched him shovel in ham, hominy, potatoes, eggs, and griddle cakes. Everything was hot enough for him. When he had finished, he wiped his face with his napkin and called for more coffee. Then he launched into the story of his evening adventure.

The fugitives never came anywhere near our house. As the patrol had reasoned, they made for the bottomland in the hopes of sneaking onto a boat and getting to New Orleans. The patrol was nine armed men on horseback and a pack of hounds. They picked up the trail after an hour or so, and in the next spotted one of the negroes climbing a tree. They left a few dogs to keep him up there, then went after the other two. These were eventually discovered hip-deep in mud at the river's edge.

They let the dogs at one, which must have been quite a spectacle, as the dogs got stuck in the mud too and had to be hauled out with ropes. The second fugitive took advantage of the confusion to get to the water, where he floundered about because he wasn't a good swimmer. Two members of the patrol went down and shot him. The one in the mud was finally pulled out like the dogs and gave up pretty readily, so they tied his hands behind his back, threw the rope over a tree limb, and went back for the one the dogs were guarding. He had tried coming down from his perch only to get one foot nearly chewed off, and was so scared they had no trouble talking him down. They put him on a horse and went back for the one they'd left tied up. Before they saw him, they heard him screaming for help. Lo and behold an alligator had discovered him and he was running around in a circle trying to keep from being eaten for dinner. The alligator got so agitated it attacked the horses, so they shot it too. And that was what Joel Borden got delivered to his door in the middle of the night, one dead negro, one with his foot nearly torn off, one just scared to death, and a dead alligator.

As he told this story, he laughed at his own wit; it had been an exciting night. Sarah stood at the sideboard listening closely, her eyes on the butter dish. I put a bland smile on my lips and kept it there, sipping my coffee during the irritating intervals of his phlegmy laughter. When he was finished he looked from Sarah to me, including us in his genial pleasure.

'I thought Joel's negroes were armed,' I said.

'No,' he replied. 'They weren't.'

16

Sarah gave me a darting look. 'Wasn't one of them Delphine's brother?' I asked.

His good humor evaporated. He looked from Sarah to me and back again. 'All you women do is talk,' he said.

As this was his first truly humorous remark of the morning, I indulged in an unladylike snort of laughter myself.

'Eben Borden,' he said to Sarah. 'Yes, he was one of them. He's the one nearly lost his foot to the dogs, and when Borden's overseer is through with him, his foot will be the least of his troubles.' He laid his hand across his chest, wincing from a sudden pain. 'So you and Delphine can quit poisoning me,' he said. 'I saved her damn brother's life.'

Sarah's face was a mask. She glanced at his cup, then took up the pot to refill it.

'You women should think about what would become of you if I wasn't here,' he said, gazing suspiciously into his half-full cup.

~

Does Sarah think about what would become of her if he were gone? How could she not? What would become of me must be her next question, as she belongs to me. She can't doubt that I would sell her; I would sell them all. I imagine it sometimes, selling them all and the house and the land, settling his debts, which are considerable. He has loans from his brother and three banks, and he has used the house as collateral for repairs on the mill. He has what my

17

father called 'planter's disease'; he keeps buying land when he hasn't the means to cultivate it. If the price of sugar falls again this year, it will hurt him, but he won't have the sense to stop planting to meet the shortfall. He doesn't know I can read an account book, but I can, and I've been looking into his for some time now. He might pull through this year if the weather is good and the price stable, but this combination is unlikely, as good weather means a better crop for everyone, which will drive the price down. I never speak to him about such things.

Though his ruin entails my own, I long for it.

Often I'm grateful that my father didn't live to see me in this place. If he knew what humiliation I suffer every day, he would be at the door with his carriage to take me home. Our home is lost, but if it were still there, still ours, though it was not half so grand as this one, with what joy would I return to its simple comforts!

Do the dead see us? Is Father weeping for me in the graveyard?

If my husband died, I think. If my husband died. But he won't. Not before it's too late for me.

~

This afternoon's game was a more straightforward one, not very original at all. Two strong boys were required to fight until one couldn't get up. The loser then received a whipping. It was an eerie scene to watch through the glass because there was no sound. Doubtless the boys were grunting and groaning, and he was urging them on, but it all looked as serene and orchestrated as a dance. I watched for several minutes. One of the boys was clearly the better fighter, though the smaller of the two. 'Come look through this glass,' I said to Sarah, 'and tell me who that smaller boy is.'

Sarah backed away as if I'd asked her to pick up a roach. 'No, missus,' she said.

'And why not?' I asked.

'I don' like that glass.'

'Have you never looked through it?'

She looked down, shaking her head slowly.

This surprised me. The glass is on the landing, pointing out of the only window in the house that faces the quarter. He had it specially mounted for this purpose, to watch the negroes at their daily business, to see if they are congregating. Sarah must pass it ten times a day.

'I'd look if I were you,' I said. 'You might see something you need to know.'

For answer she took another step back.

'Or do you already know everything you need to know?' I said, turning back to the glass.

I was right. The taller boy lay facedown in the dirt, his legs drawn up under him, trying to lift himself up like a baby learning to walk. The victor stood before him, unsmiling, sweating. In the shadow of the tree I saw him, bending over to put down his Bible and take up his stick. As he turned toward the fighters, he said something to the victor, who looked up boldly at the house, directly at me, or so it seemed. I backed away from the window, stunned, momentarily as guilty as a child caught stealing candy.

19

Sarah had passed into my room, where her baby was whinning. Why should I feel guilty? I thought.

~

When he was courting me, he was mysterious, and I took his aloofness for sensitivity. He was a man who required his linen to be scented and spotless, who could not stay long in the city because the stench from the sewers offended him. When he visited our cottage, I had the parlor scrubbed out and scented with rosewater and vetiver, and my own hair washed with chamomile. He never failed to comment on the agreeable atmosphere in our rooms.

'If he's fastidious,' my Aunt Lelia said, when she heard of our engagement, 'you'd best have my Sarah. She's country-bred, used to country houses. She's the best house-keeper I've ever had, though she's not eighteen. She hates the town because she says the dirt walks in the house every time the door is opened. I will give her to you as my wedding gift.'

And that was how Sarah came to this house, six weeks before I did, commissioned to ready it for my arrival. My husband was impressed with her and wrote my aunt himself to thank her for this 'prize'; his house had never been so well arranged.

I wonder how my aunt could have dealt my happiness such a blow. Did she imagine my husband was different from hers? Did she think that because I was young and pretty, I was proof against the temptations presented by Sarah?

20

Or was she only desperate? I learned later, much too late, that my uncle had lost his head when a free man of color offered to buy Sarah so that he might free her and marry her. The free man was in my uncle's employ, overseeing the construction of an addition to their house, and he fancied that he was in love with Sarah. My uncle fired the man, who straightaway sued for damages. This so enraged my uncle that he had Sarah tied up in the kitchen and whipped her himself, in front of the cook. That was when my aunt began to look for someplace to get rid of her.

The day I arrived here, she was standing on the porch with the others, Delphine and Bam, the butler, who is gone now, and Rose, who was just a child, supposedly of use to Delphine in the kitchen. 'Here we are,' he said, helping me down from the carriage. 'Your new home.'

The house is in the West Indies style, flush to the ground with brick columns below and wooden above. The upstairs gallery is wide and closed in by a rail, but the porch below is open to whatever stumbles across the brick floor, lizards, snakes, and every kind of beetle the swamps can disgorge. Casement doors open across the front, upstairs and down, framed by batten shutters that are only closed in hurricanes or at the threat of revolt. I went ahead of my husband to greet the minimal staff. Delphine gave me a quick curtsy and an open, curious look. I asked her name, greeted her, was introduced to Rose, who couldn't raise her eyes from my skirt. Bam, a lanky, long-faced, dark-skinned fellow, dressed in a coat that was too narrow in the shoulders and short at the sleeves, gave me a formal bow and said, 'Welcome, missus.'

21

'This is Bam,' my husband said. I nodded, turning to Sarah. I knew who she was, that she was my aunt's wedding gift. Her appearance was pleasing, tall, slender, light-skinned, neatly dressed, excellent posture. Her hands were folded over her apron. She acknowledged me with something between a bow and a curtsy, but she wasn't looking at me at all. She was looking past me, with an expression of sullen expectation, at my husband.

~

Father never kept more than fifteen field hands and their families. Each year, depending on his crop, he hired extra hands for the picking and ginning. Cotton is a less finicky crop than cane and doesn't require the bulk of the harvesting and milling to be done all at once under the pressure of a hard freeze. Cane-growers spend Christmas in a panic and the negroes don't have their party and holiday until after the new year.

Whenever Father went to the hiring barn, the negroes pressed around him and begged him to take them on. They all knew they would be better housed and fed on his farm than on their masters' grand plantations, and that they would have a full day of rest once a week. Our New Year's party was famous among them, and once hired, they shouted and slapped one another on the back, congratulating themselves on the feast they would enjoy together.

I remember standing at the window to watch their procession come up from the quarter. The torches were like flaming birds swooping and soaring over their heads. Father

22

stood on the porch with his basket of envelopes, each with a name on the front and a crisp bill inside. There was much laughter, joking, and singing. When each one had received his gift, Father cried out, 'And now for the feast,' and led them to the barn, which was all festooned with greenery, with long tables set out, draped in bright red cloths and laden with beef and pork roasts, chickens, turkeys, bowls of greens and mashed potatoes, all manner of fruit, breads, puddings, pies, candies, and, along the walls, barrels of sweet wine and tafia. I was allowed to go with him and see the bustle as they took their places and began piling their plates. Later, in my bed, I heard the first strains of the fiddles and the scraping and shouting as they pulled the tables to the side and began the dancing which lasted late into the night. In the morning everyone slept late and Father arrived at the table as we were finishing our breakfast. 'I believe the negroes enjoyed their festivities,' he would say, sitting down to cold coffee and leftover eggs.

Father was strict and fair. None of our people could marry off the farm, indeed they could never leave it unless they had some compelling reason, and visits by negroes from the neighboring farms and plantations were strictly forbidden. He didn't allow them to work garden patches of their own, as he said it gave them a notion of independence and divided their loyalty, so that they might take more interest in their own patch than in the farm. In order to have peace and harmony, he said, the negroes must recognize that the farm is their provider and protector, that it gives them every good thing, food, medical attention, clean housing, heat in winter, friends and family, that it is the place they come from and where they will be valued and cared for until they die.

He would have no overseer. He had the same driver for fifteen years. He used the whip sparingly and stood by while the driver administered the sentence, for he said it was wrong that any master be seen raising a whip himself; it demeaned him in the eyes of those who stood by.

I was never allowed, as most planters' children were, to play with the negro children on our farm. Father considered it a perverse practice that resulted in a coarsening of the master's children and was the source of inappropriate expectations in the negroes, who must feel themselves the equals of their playmates. This familiarity could breed naught but contempt, Father maintained, and so I learned to make companions of my dolls.

Above all, Father deplored the practice of some of his neighbors, who paraded about the town with their mulatto children in tow. That these men were often to be seen singing in church on Sunday morning was one more reason, Father maintained, to have nothing to do with religion. Religion was for the negroes, he said; it was their solace and consolation, as they were ours.

I didn't know, as a girl, how remarkable Father was. When my mother complained that his death was no accident, I took her charge to be the product of her grief. But now I think he must have had a world of enemies. When our home was gone and we moved to the city, I learned that Father, who was so strong, loving, stern, and fair, was all that stood between my innocent happiness and chaos.

I sometimes think Sarah blames me for her fate, though I had nothing to do with it. She sealed it herself shortly after I arrived by getting pregnant. The father was my husband's butler, Bam. I had noticed that he could not keep his eyes off her when Sarah passed through the room and I was not surprised to learn that they hoped to marry. She told me first and I saw nothing against it. She entreated me to tell my husband, as she feared he wouldn't agree to the match. This was when she still talked and behaved like a normal servant, asking for permission, eager to please. I agreed to inform my husband of her request. It seemed an advantageous match to me, as it would serve to strengthen their loyalty to the property. These marriages the negroes make are not legal, but they set great store by them.

I wonder now how I could have been such a fool. My husband's reaction to this news was to leap up from his desk, bellowing like a bull. He bid me send Sarah to him at once and when she came, he pulled her inside by her arm and commenced slapping and hitting her until she was flat on the floor, begging him to stop. It was not to be borne, he swore, that he should be treated in this fashion in his own house. When I spoke a word on her behalf, he pushed me out of the room and slammed the door in my face. Then, while I was standing there, listening to Sarah's pleas and his curses, I understood everything. Sarah had resisted him all those weeks when I wasn't there, and now she had tried to outmaneuver him, but she never would again.

My husband called upon Mr Sutter, who appeared in the

dining room just before dinner with two brutish field hands at his side. The three of them dragged Bam off to the quarter, howling that he never had been whipped in his life and would not be whipped now; he would kill himself first. Later we learned that he escaped his captors briefly, took up an ax from a stump and threatened to cut off his own hand to render himself worthless to his master. The boys rushed him, and in the ensuing struggle one of them got a deep gash in his leg, which so enraged Mr Sutter that he beat Bam near to death. It was six weeks before he was recovered enough to be transported to the city, where he was sold.

Sarah's baby, a boy, was taken from her as soon as it was born and sent out to nurse at my brother-in-law's plantation upriver, with the understanding that when he was old enough to work, he would be sold, and the profit, after his board was deducted, divided between the brothers. Sarah wept, pleaded, then grew silent and secretive. My husband was pleased with himself, though he'd been forced to sell a valuable negro at a loss. When the dealers saw Bam's scars, they took him for a troublesome fellow and lowered their offers accordingly. By the end of that year, Sarah was pregnant with Walter.

~

Joel Borden stopped here on his way to the town, with a bag of doves he'd shot himself and a fresh ham, not something we need, as we've pigs to spare. My husband asked him to stay for dinner and he agreed. Though the men all talk behind his back, Joel is such an easy fellow they treat him like a friend to his face. And, of course, when they go to town, they are quick to look him up, as he knows where all the parties and dances are and is welcome in the best houses for his charm and wit. Once a year he gives a party at his plantation, Rivière, and there is a line of carriages up the river road for a solid day. I attended once, the first year I came here.

Now, as I came into the dining room, I found Joel sprawled over a chair facing the windows, a glass of bourbon on the table next to him. My husband was not in the room. Sarah came in with a stack of plates to lay the table. Joel looked round, and, seeing me, leaped to his feet, holding out his hands to take my own. 'Manon,' he said, looking me up and down, 'you haven't changed. No, wait, I think you are a little more beautiful.'

But I *have* changed, so much that I hardly remember how to carry on trivial banter, though once I was proficient. 'You look well, Joel,' was all I said. He's a handsome man in an indolent, good-natured way. He has only enough energy to seek his own pleasure continually; everything else is too much for him.

'I saw your mother last week,' he said, 'and I promised I would look in on you before my return.'

He has a bevy of old ladies who adore him; my mother is one. She wanted Joel to marry me, though we all knew it was impossible because Joel needs money and I have none. He played at courting me briefly, then moved on to another available beauty. When he decides to marry, he will choose someone rich, possibly older than he is, but for now poor girls always come with doting mothers, who ply him with dinner and sherry or port. I wonder how much longer he can hold out without selling something.

'Please tell her I am well,' I said. He released my hands, puzzled by my unresponsiveness. Then the reason for it came banging in the door, brandishing a bottle and addressing a barking order to Sarah. He pounced on Joel with fake geniality, on the subject of a dog he must see before he left. I followed Sarah to the door and whispered to her, 'Tell Delphine to serve a blancmange for dessert.' She nodded, and went out. My husband was opening the wine bottle, a particularly fine claret which he highly recommended to our guest. Though I don't usually drink in the afternoon, something in his excitement at having company made me decide to join them. I took three glasses from the sideboard and brought them to the table. My husband gave me a quick glance, skepticism combined with surprise. He thought Joel had stopped because he was grateful that his negroes weren't all dead, but I knew he had come, as he said, because he promised my mother he would. She had sent a letter the day after the patrol, full of the idiotic rumors circulating in town: Joel's three negroes had become ten, armed with rifles and machetes and intent on joining a band who lived in the swamp downriver. I had not had time to respond to this jittery letter.

My husband wanted to talk about cane, and so he did, all through the meal. He went on about the press and the bagasse and the market and the weather until I thought I would faint from boredom. All Joel knows about sugar is what his overseer tells him. He and I drank most of the wine while my husband entertained us with estimates of how much time and money he could save if he had the newest mill, which is more efficient than any previously invented and more expensive than any planter can afford. Sarah came in and out, bringing new dishes, removing plates. My husband neither spoke to her nor looked at her, nor did Joel, who was occupied in sending me sly remarks about a new mill that ran on bourbon, or another that actually ran on sugar, an invention long overdue. He is so droll, and since he kept filling my glass, I was soon feeling relaxed and gay, as I always was in the old days. My husband didn't appear to object; it is such a rarity for him to see me smile. When the bottle was empty, he excused himself to go off for another. Joel took my hand in his and said, 'Manon, why don't you come to town for a visit? It's so dull without you there.'

'You have no idea what dullness is,' I said. 'You've no experience of it.' At these words my husband returned, carrying two bottles, his timing so appropriate that I was overcome with laughter. Joel laughed too, at his host's expense. My husband regarded us hopefully. 'I've an excellent port,' he said.

'I shall fall off my horse before I get to False River,' Joel exclaimed.

Then my husband pressed him to stay the night, but there was never any hope of that. I could see the wasted afternoon through Joel's eyes, napping or reading or looking at dogs when he could be arriving in town in time for an elegant supper, followed by gambling and flirting. What would it be like to be married to such a man, I thought, to enter on his arm a room full of envious girls? A familiar gloom descended upon me. With Joel, I would have had children.

Sarah came in with the blancmange, which Joel, smiling at me, pronounced his favorite. He ate an entire one once at my mother's house, so it is a joke between us. Sarah set the dish down before me and my husband directed her to bring the port glasses. As she passed behind him on her way to the sideboard, she cast him a furtive look; she wasn't happy about something. Then we heard a clattering in the hall, the door flew open, and Walter rushed in.

He was barefoot, wearing only white pantaloons and a red kerchief around his neck. He dashed around the table, his spindly arms raised over his head, his eyes rolling wildly, singing something he apparently thought was a song, though it had neither tune nor sense. He stopped at my husband's chair only long enough to shriek and push himself off against the table, then he careened past me and threw himself at Joel, grasping him by the waist and burying his curly head in his waistcoat.

A good many things happened at once. My husband rose from his seat, shouting at Sarah to take the boy from the room. Walter lifted his face and began gibbering at Joel, who turned to me with an expression of astonishment and asked, 'What have we here?' Then, as Sarah pulled the boy away by the arm, I saw Joel take in the mad creature's marked resemblance to my husband. I believe his mouth dropped open. My husband understood that Joel understood, which infuriated him. He pushed back his chair and followed Sarah and the screaming child, directing slaps at one and then the other. The boy took the blow on the back of his head and howled, so enraged that he lost his footing. Sarah scooped him up by the waist and took him, kicking and screaming, from the room. My husband slammed the door behind them and came back to the table.

I could feel Joel's eyes upon me and my cheeks burned with shame. I heard my father's voice, reminding me that a gentleman never raises his voice to a servant in public. What would he have thought of a man who strikes a child at a dinner party? My husband sat down in a huff and busied himself pouring out the port. An awful silence enveloped the table, and I could think of no way to break it. At last Joel said, 'Are you going to serve me that dessert, Manon, or is it just there to tempt my appetite?'

'Of course,' I said, taking up the spoon. 'Just pass me your plate.' Then my husband asked Joel about the shooting at his place, a question which genuinely interested our guest, as he thinks the only pleasure in country living is the hunting, so they began to talk, and we went on as if nothing had happened, as if Joel wasn't going back to town with a story that would amuse his bachelor friends: Manon Gaudet has no children, but her husband is not childless. It was a common enough tale; no one would think it a paradox. My only comfort was that I knew Joel would say nothing to my mother.

⁓

After Joel left, my husband went to see Mr Sutter and I went to my room. I was still flushed and tipsy from the wine, but my good humor had been thoroughly destroyed. As we stood on the porch bidding our guest farewell, my husband had insisted on passing his arm around my waist, and there was nothing I could do but bear it until Joel was out of sight. There we were, a loving couple, waving and smiling as our guest turned his horse toward the town, no doubt eager to be done with us and our sham of a marriage. When he was out of earshot, I removed my husband's hand and said, 'Won't Joel have some amusing stories to tell when he gets to town?'

'What are you talking about?' he said.

'He can tell all my friends I live with a man whose bastard son runs wild in the dining room and who strikes his servants in public. That should paint an edifying picture of the choice I've made.'

He made no answer, but strode off toward the quarter.

In my room, I threw myself across my bed and wept. I cried until I fell asleep. When I woke, Sarah was there nursing her baby, her eyes closed, a dreamy expression on her face.

'Did you send Walter in to get even with me or with him?' I asked.

Her eyes snapped open. I turned my face away.

'He just snuck in,' she said.

~

I stayed in my room all evening. Sarah brought my supper on a tray, but I could scarcely eat it. Just after dark it began to rain and a wind picked up, rattling the shutters against the house. I changed into my nightclothes. After Sarah had brushed my hair, I sent her and the baby away for the night. Then I lay upon the bed thinking about Joel, about the look on his face when he turned to me over Walter's babbling head and said, 'What have we here?' Was it pity? I couldn't bear that. I thought about my husband, and these thoughts, never warm, were like icy jets darting about in my brain. I could hear him moving about downstairs. I dozed, woke again to hear him climbing the stairs. He is heavy-footed. It's hard to figure how one man walking can make as much noise as he does. He passed my door and went on to his own room. The rain had stopped, the wind had swept the clouds away, and moonlight streamed in through the window. My head ached from the wine and my throat was parched. I slipped out of bed, poured myself a glass of water, then went to look out the window, just for something to do. I felt I wouldn't sleep again for years. It was still windy, the trees waved their upper branches as if they were calling me outside. I looked up at the clear sky, the glittering stars, then I looked down and discovered, near the foot of an oak, a man. Startled, I stepped away from the window. Had he seen me? I pulled the curtain in front of me and looked out past it cautiously, though my room was dark and it was unlikely that he could see me. It was a negro, dressed in a white shirt and loose breeches that whipped around in the wind. He was standing very still, his arms crossed, gazing up at the house. I couldn't make out his features. Was he one of ours?

I crept back to the bed and pulled the coverlet over me. He had no business coming up to the house after nightfall.

If I woke my husband he would go out and chase the fellow back where he belonged.

Then I thought that perhaps my husband knew he was there. Perhaps he was a sentry, posted to protect us from yet another rumor of revolt. I waited, breathing shallowly, as if the man might hear me. After a while I got up and crept back to the window. I got on my hands and knees and peeped through the bottom pane.

He was gone.

～

I took a spoonful of tincture to get back to sleep and woke up feeling dead, unable to move my limbs. I heard the clock strike and knew I must get up and prepare myself to appear in the dining room, a thought that made my stomach turn. I lay on my side clutching my abdomen and panting for a few moments, then, as the sensation passed, I managed to get to my feet. I washed my face at the basin, trying not to see my reflection in the mirror, but I did see it, and it frightened me. I rang the bell, waited a moment, and rang it again. Shortly I heard Sarah's step on the stair. 'For God's sake, help me dress,' I said when she came in.

She opened the armoire and pulled out my blue lawn morning dress, the lightest, least-confining thing I own. 'Yes,' I said. 'Put it right over my shift; there's no time for the corset.' I drank a little water and collapsed at the dresser. 'Just pin up the braid,' I said. She took the brush to the front and secured the back with a dozen pins, while I rubbed a little rouge into my cheeks. 'What is wrong with my eyes?'

I said, for they were red-rimmed and staring, the pupils like black saucers in a band of pale blue. We heard the bell to the dining room. 'I best go,' Sarah said.

'Go on,' I told her. 'Tell him I'll be down directly.' When she was gone, I pulled on my shoes and fastened a tucker in the bodice of the dress. 'A cup of coffee will bring me round,' I said. Abruptly I remembered the man, but I had no time to think about him. I hurried out across the landing and down the stairs, clutching the rail like a woman in a swoon. As I approached the door, I could hear the clatter of dishes, the steady scraping of my husband's fork against his plate. When I went in, he was sopping up gravy with a piece of bread. He looked up at me without stopping. I took my seat, turned my cup over, adjusted my skirt.

'Are you ill?' he asked by way of greeting.

Sarah came between us with the coffee pot. Blessed coffee, I thought as the fragrant steam rose from the cup. I took a careful sip before answering. 'I slept poorly,' I said.

'It is because you take no exercise,' he said. I waved away the plate of eggs Sarah held out before me. 'Just toasted bread,' I said.

'And you eat nothing,' he continued. 'It's no wonder you've made yourself ill.' He shoved in the last of his dripping bread, smacking his lips appreciatively. 'More coffee,' he said to Sarah.

I dipped my toast in my cup. My head was beginning to clear a little. As Sarah leaned across him, he gave her a perplexed inspection. 'Send Walter to me,' he said.

'Oh, please, no,' I exclaimed.

'What objection could you have?' he said coldly.

'My head is bursting,' I complained.

Sarah set the urn back on the sideboard.

'Send him to me,' he said again.

When she went out, he said to me, 'Joel Borden is right. You should go to town and visit your mother. Why don't you write to her?'

'My place is here,' I said. Then the door opened and Walter was upon us, followed by Sarah, who was making a study of the carpet. Walter was wearing only a slip, such as the field children wear. It was too big for him and hung off one shoulder; the skirt came nearly to his ankles. My husband pushed his chair back from the table and called the creature, holding out his arms to him, but the child just ran around the table, as is his wont, babbling and giving high-pitched shrieks for no reason. At length he passed close enough for his father to grab him. 'Hold still,' he said, struggling with his squirming catch. 'Hold still, hold still, and I will give you some muffin.' He pinned the boy's arms behind his back with one hand and with the other reached out to Sarah, demanding 'Muffin, muffin.' She quickly broke up a few pieces onto a plate and set it before him. This got the boy's attention. He began a low crooning, straining his head toward the plate. My husband took up a bit and pressed it to the child's lips, quieting him momentarily. 'How old is he now?' he asked Sarah.

'He seven,' she said.

He ran his hand through the boy's wild red hair. 'Doesn't anyone ever comb his hair?' he asked.

'He won' stand for it.'

My husband looked into Walter's mad face, feeding him

another bit of muffin to keep his attention. 'No,' he said approvingly. 'Why should he?'

Walter's eyes opened wide; he brought his face close to his father's, swallowed the last bite, and shouted 'Poo-poo, poo-poo' at the top of his lungs. Sarah jumped away from the sideboard, grabbed the horrid creature by one arm, and dragged him toward the doors. 'He have to go out,' she said. When the doors were open, he scurried across the bricks into the azaleas and squatted down in the dirt.

'A charming child,' I observed.

Sarah closed the doors and resumed her post at the sideboard. 'More coffee,' I said.

My husband looked abashed. It delighted me to see him trying to make his dull brain work over the problem presented by this monster he has brought among us. 'So he can speak?' he said.

'Delphine taught him that.'

'Can he say anything else?'

'Maybe Delphine understand him sometime.'

'But you don't.'

Sarah studied his face for a moment without speaking. Then she said, 'Delphine say he don't hear.'

'He's deaf,' my husband said softly, as if a deep revelation had just come to him. Then, tersely, 'I shall send for Dr Landry today.'

~

I rarely visit in town because I can't bear my mother's prying into the state of my marriage, her constant insinuations about my failure to conceive a child. For a few years I didn't mind, I even felt a mild curiosity about it myself; as I explained to Mother, it wasn't for lack of trying. She cherished the hope that the fault was with my husband, and I foolishly did too, until Walter was born. Then I knew the reason. In a way, Walter *is* the reason, but I could speak to no one about it. In the fifth year of my marriage, Mother and my husband consulted a doctor reputed to have helped other childless couples, and then there was no living with either of them until I agreed to be examined by this man. So I went to town and, at the appointed time, presented myself at the offices of Dr Gabriel Sanchez.

He was a small, swarthy man, his thin hair gray at the temples, his eyes slightly crossed; perhaps one eye was only weak. I was required to undress behind a screen, wrapped in sheets by a nurse, then partially unwrapped, my modesty consulted to absurd lengths. The physical examination was extremely repugnant, but I did not object to it. I thought if I would submit, the doctor might find some physical reason for my failure to conceive, thereby freeing me of my detested conjugal duties, and also putting an end to my mother's tiresome queries. When it was over, a girl was sent in to help me dress and I was escorted into the office where Dr Sanchez awaited me. It was a surprisingly sunny room. The floor was covered with a rush mat; the chairs were in summer covers. The doctor motioned me into one facing his desk, which was really a table covered with papers, books, and, oddly enough, a potted geranium. As I took my seat I noticed a large wrought-iron cage hanging from a chain near the open window in which two canaries hopped about. During our conversation, one of these birds sang plaintively.

He began well. He told me that he was obliged to ask me a number of personal questions, and that I could be assured my answers would not travel beyond the walls of his office, that in particular he would not repeat anything I said to my mother or my husband. I found the darting, unfocused looks he gave me reassuring, and I made up my mind to tell him whatever he wanted to know. I wanted to enlist him on my side. He asked about my monthly discharges, were they regular, copious, clotted, or clear, attended by pain or swelling? He asked about my general health, my diet, how much riding I did, if I ever suffered from dizziness or fainting spells. As my health has always been excellent, I answered these questions readily, nor could he have been much surprised at my responses. He listened closely, occasionally making a note in a leather-bound book he had open before him.

Then he questioned me about my marriage, and in particular about my sexual congress with my husband. How often did our relations take place, did I experience pain, was there ever bleeding afterward? He asked most delicately if I was certain that my husband ejaculated into my womb, a question which made me laugh, though I could not look at him and felt a hot flush rising in my cheeks. 'I apologize for being so indelicate,' he said, 'but I have known cases of infertility caused by inadequate knowledge on the part of the husband.'

'My husband knows very well how babies are made, I assure you,' I said coldly.

He fiddled with his pen and made no answer. I looked past him at the window where the bird was singing. There was a plantain tree just outside with a big bruised purple pod of unripe fruit hanging from it. One of the leaves lay across the windowsill like a fold of impossibly bright satin. I thought of my husband's embraces, so urgent and disagreeable, his kneading and sucking at my breasts until the nipples hurt, his fingers probing between my legs, his harsh breath in my face.

'I see no physical reason why you can't have a child,' the doctor said at last.

'No,' I agreed. 'There is no physical reason.'

'Do you want children, Mrs Gaudet?'

I gave this question thought. I had assumed I would have children, the question of whether I wanted them had never occurred to me. What sort of woman doesn't want children? Dr Sanchez waited upon my answer, but he had a calm, patient air about him, as if he wouldn't mind waiting forever. Suppose I had married a man like him, I thought, a man who knew everything about women's bodies and was never impatient. I arrived at my answer. 'No,' I said.

He nodded, pressing his lips together. He had known all along. 'Do you fear the pain of childbirth?'

'No,' I said.

'Perhaps you feel anxiety about the disfigurement of pregnancy?'

'That passes, surely,' I said.

'There is some other reason,' he concluded.

'Yes,' I said. He produced a handkerchief, picked up a pair of eyeglasses that lay upon a stack of books on his desk, and began methodically rubbing the lenses. 'It is because I despise my husband,' I said.

He looked up at me briefly, but without surprise, then returned his attention to his eyeglasses. 'Unhappy marriages still produce children,' he said.

'Perhaps they are not unhappy enough,' I replied.

'Has it occurred to you that a child might be a comfort to you in your suffering?'

'I am not in need of comforting,' I said.

He put the glasses down and gave me his full, unfocused attention. 'Did you love your husband when you married him?' he asked.

'I hardly knew him. Ours was considered an advantageous match.'

'And how did he earn your enmity?'

'Well, let me think,' I said. 'Would the fact that the servant I brought to the marriage has borne him a son, and that this creature is allowed to run loose in the house like a wild animal, would that be, in your view, sufficient cause for a wife to despise her husband?'

He shrugged. 'Mrs Gaudet, there are many such cases. This cannot be unknown to you.'

'That is precisely my grievance,' I explained. 'That it is common.'

'Why not sell the girl?'

'No. He would only find another. And this one suits me. She hates him as much as I do.'

I saw a flicker of sympathy cross his expression, but I didn't think it was for me. He was feeling pity for my husband, trapped between two furies. 'Well,' he said. 'God willing, you will have a child. You're young, in good health.'

'That's what I fear,' I said. 'That's why I consented to see you. I want you to tell my husband that I cannot bear children. That it endangers my life even to try.'

'You want me to lie? I would never do that.'

'Not to save my life?' I said desperately.

'Your life is not in danger.'

Against my will, tears sprang to my eyes. I felt one of my headaches tightening across my forehead. I drew my handkerchief from my sleeve and pressed it against each eye. Dr Sanchez was speaking, but I could hardly make out what he was saying through the awful red clamp of pain. It was something about a child, my child, who would secure my husband's affections to me. 'Can't you at least give me something for these headaches?' I blurted out, interrupting him.

He paused, midsentence, as if to draw attention to my rudeness, but I no longer cared what he thought of me. 'And something to make me sleep,' I added.

'Yes,' he said softly. 'That much I can do for you.'

∽

While we were at dinner, a boy arrived with a note from Dr Landry saying there was cholera at Overton and he could not come to us until supper. 'You must tell him our case is not urgent,' I said. 'He will be exhausted if he has to make the trip back there before morning.'

'Why should he?' my husband said. 'He can stay here and have a decent night's sleep, instead of being up a hundred times in the night to bleed hysterical negroes.'

'You wouldn't say so if they were your own negroes,' I observed.

'If they were my negroes, I'd move the quarter up from that swamp they're in at Overton, and there would be no cholera, as there is none here.'

This is one of his favorite pastimes, pointing out that everyone's troubles are their own fault and if the whole world would only submit to his excellent management, it would be an earthly paradise. It bores me past endurance. I pushed my plate away and got up from the table. 'I must speak to Delphine about supper,' I said. As I went out, Sarah was coming in with a plate of rice cakes. She had a smirk on her face, pleased with herself, I thought, because Walter was going to get the doctor's attention. I went through the house, out the back door, across the yard, and in at the kitchen. Delphine had her back to me, rolling out some dough at the table. The fire was up, the room stifling. I threw myself down in a chair, startling her momentarily. 'It's hell in here,' I said. 'How can you stand it?'

'Can't cook without fire,' she said, continuing her rolling.

'Give me a glass of water before I faint.'

She wiped her hands on her apron and went to the pump. I seldom go into the kitchen, but whenever I do, in spite of the heat, I feel more at ease than in my own room. Delphine is the only person in this house I trust at all. She reminds me of Peek, my mother's cook; they are both small, very dark, lively, jittery, but sensible at bottom. She brought me the water glass, wiping the rim with her apron. 'They's flour on the glass,' she said.

'I don't care,' I said, gulping it down. She took up her pin again. 'The doctor is coming to supper tonight,' I said. 'It's too hot to eat, but he probably will. He's a big man.'

'Doctor got a good appetite,' she agreed.

'Get a ham from the smokehouse,' I said. 'Just serve it cold. Cold potatoes dressed with vinegar, biscuits, pickled peaches, and applesauce. What pie are you making?'

'Rhubarb.'

'That's so plain,' I said.

'I can mix in some strawberries.'

'All right,' I said. 'Serve some whipped cream with it. It will have to do.' I went through my keys. 'Here's the smokehouse key,' I said, laying it on the end of the table. 'Send it back with Sarah when you're done.'

'Yes, missus,' she said.

I thought I would get up to go, but I felt so languid I didn't move. I looked out the door at the yard. A chicken walked by. Everything felt peaceful; then I recalled why.

'Where's Walter?' I said.

'Out running 'round,' she said.

'Is that safe?'

'Rose look after him,' she said.

'It's not him I'm worried about. It's the property.'

Delphine draped her dough over the pie pan and turned to look into a pot on the hearth.

'Make sure he's inside by supper,' I said. 'The doctor is going to examine him.'

'Yes, missus,' she said.

I got up and stretched, then wandered out into the yard. I couldn't take the hot kitchen another minute. I was thinking about the man, but I wasn't going to say anything to Delphine about him. Perhaps he was her lover. I walked out to the oak where I had seen him and looked among the roots for any shoe prints or anything he might have dropped, but there was nothing. I stood exactly where I thought he had stood and looked up at the house. I could see my bedroom window – one curtain was fluttering half outside in the breeze – and my husband's window as well. When I looked at the kitchen yard I could see right into the open door. By turning a little, I could see the top of the mill and the dirt road running to the quarter. Quite an excellent command post.

I looked back at my own window. The curtains seemed to be moving against something heavy, then they parted and Sarah appeared, holding her baby. She saw me at once, but she didn't start or turn away. She just stood there, her dress half-opened, looking down at me coolly. She's a nerveless creature, I thought. There really is something inhuman about her. After a few moments I grew weary of looking at her and went back into the house.

~

Dr Landry is a walking newspaper. He knows everything that is happening from St. Francisville to Pointe à la Hache. All through supper he dispensed interesting gossip, yet he still managed to eat nearly half a ham. The cholera at Overton is confined to the quarters; of sixty-three taken, sixteen have died. It is worse in New Orleans, and there is yellow fever there as well. The hospital is full, the hotels

45

empty. Mrs. Pemberly, near Clinton, has scarlet fever and is so weak the doctor does not expect her to live. The lawsuit her daughter-in-law brought against her son has proved successful and she anticipates the loss of half her property. Two negroes have drowned in False River. They had passes to visit their families and, seeing a skiff in the weeds, must have thought to arrive with a fish dinner, but the boat proved leaky and they turned dinner for the fishes. Two runaways were captured at St Francisville, walking around drunk in broad daylight. There was a fire at Mr Winthrop's gin at Greenwood, set by his own negroes. One of the culprits informed on the others and escaped beating. The fire consumed eighty bales of cotton as well. There are so many rumors of planned uprisings at Bayou Sara that the authorities have banned all church meetings of any kind, as it seems one of the preachers may be responsible for inciting the negroes. One story has it that there are three hundred runaways hidden in the low country near there and that they plan to march down the river road killing every white person they find.

'They would come right past here,' my husband exclaimed on hearing this.

'That they would,' Dr Landry agreed. 'If the rumors are true.'

'I will inform my meeting,' my husband said, solemn and pompous as an ass. This is how rumors turn into dead negroes.

After supper Dr Landry agreed to examine Walter, who was described as 'a boy we have here.' My husband expressed the hope that some use might be made of the child as a servant, which was entirely news to me. My heart raced with anger, then I imagined Walter pitching dishes out the window and dumping mashed potatoes on the carpet, a thought I found so amusing it calmed me down. They agreed the examination would take place in my husband's office, and Sarah was dispatched to bring the creature there. I made my excuses to the gentlemen, and said good night to the doctor at the dining room door, but instead of going to my room, I went back to the table. After a few minutes, Sarah came in to clear up. She was doubtless vexed to see me still sitting there.

'Pour me a glass of that port the gentlemen found so edifying,' I said, and she did. Then I sat quietly for some time, drinking the port and thinking over the news the doctor had brought us. What interested me most was the success of Sally Pemberly's lawsuit against her husband. She divorced him some years ago, because he was so cruel even the servants pitied her. He then ran up large gambling debts, bankrupting himself as well as his family. Sally sued to have her marriage portion, which was considerable, exempted from his creditors and restored to her. By some miracle, she has won. Now she has her own income and she is free of her detestable husband. Fortunate woman!

~

I woke up with a start, thinking someone was standing next to my bed, but there was no one there. Had I heard a sound? The room was black. I could make out the curtains at the window but little else. At once I remembered the man. I pulled back the net and sat on the edge of the bed, groggy but determined, shaking my head to clear it. Then I went to the window.

It was like looking into the inkwell. I could make out the shape of the oak, but only as texture, like black velvet against black silk. Was there something among the roots? I dropped down to my knees, as I thought my white shift, my light hair, made me visible, and gazed long and hard. Still my eyes failed to penetrate the darkness. Did something move, there, near the house? Listen, I told myself and I closed my eyes, listening as what had seemed like silence unraveled into different sounds, the buzz of insects, the clock in the hall, something scratching in the wall, the rustling of leaves and branches, and then, just beyond my own heartbeat, not near or loud, but sudden and unmistakable, the sound of a rifle shot.

My eyes flew open. I jumped up and ran for the bedroom door, but I tripped over a footstool and fell headlong across the carpet. As I got to my feet, I heard a shout from outside, then my husband's voice, cursing. I opened my bedroom door just as his door was opened. A lamp sputtered, someone came out into the hall. It was Sarah. I stepped behind the door, laying my cheek against the wood, listening as she hurried toward the landing.

Another door opened, the doctor's. He spoke to her, she answered, but I couldn't make out what they said. There was more light, the heavy sound of my husband's boots, then his voice. 'They've set the mill on fire,' he said, and Dr Landry replied, 'I'll dress and join you.' My husband was halfway down the stairs. 'Stay in your bed,' he called back. 'There are hands enough.'

How could the mill be on fire? I'd just been looking toward it. I felt my way to my dresser, lit the lamp, and went to the window. It was true. There were no flames, but there was a deep red glow to the blackness in that direction. I heard shouts downstairs, my husband appeared on the lawn, running, and from the quarter two men bearing torches came running to meet him. The doctor's door opened again, his footsteps faded as he hurried downstairs. After a few moments he too appeared below me, walking briskly toward the fire.

My heart smote me. It was this way that night: the sounds of doors opening and closing, the clatter of boots on the stairs. But it was different too. It was clear and cold. When I woke up and looked out my window, I could see the flames and smoke billowing up above the trees. I never did see Father leave the house, and I never did see him again. I heard Mother's voice, then a man's voice I didn't recognize, more doors closing, someone riding away. I leaped from my bed and ran into the hall calling for Mother, but she didn't answer. I found her in the parlor with our house-maid Celeste; they had only one lamp lit between them and the room was cold. Mother's crochet hook glinted amid the lace she was frantically working. Celeste was darning a sock. I wanted to throw myself in Mother's lap, but I knew she would scold me. 'What is happening?' I said. Mother looked up, hollow-eyed, her mouth in a grim line, shadows from the lamp playing over her cheeks. She's frightened, I thought. She's more frightened than I am.

'They have murdered him,' she said.

'Father!' I cried and ran to the door.

'Manon,' Mother shouted, jumping to her feet. 'Don't go out there.' She came to me and took me in her arms and I wept. I couldn't understand what had happened. 'The driver has gone for your uncle,' Mother said, 'and we must stay inside until he comes.'

That night I slept in Mother's bed. In the morning she refused to get up, refused to eat, sobbed and muttered wild accusations by turns. 'She mad with grief,' Celeste said.

Late in the afternoon my uncle arrived and I was allowed to leave the house. 'Stay away from the quarter,' he said, 'and stay away from the gin.' All night I had wanted to run, and as soon as I was outside I did run, as hard and fast as I could, across the lawn and down the road to the river landing. I wanted to keep running forever, but I came to the end of the dock. The water swirled at my feet, the wind lifted my hair. No steamer was in sight. I raised my arms above my head and called out 'Father, Father,' in a transport of suffering. But of course there was no answer; Father was gone.

What happened then? A blackness suffused my memory. I was sick for some time. But before that.

Before that, I turned back and saw two negro boys standing at the edge of the dock, watching me curiously. They were dressed in rags, their feet bare. One wore a rough jacket made of quilted sacking, the other had fashioned a cape from what looked like a scrap of horse blanket which he held tight around his thin shoulders. I judged them to be twelve or thirteen, my age, though I was several inches taller than they were. I wasn't afraid of them. I didn't think I had seen them before.

I approached the boys. When I was close, the taller of them said, 'Your pappy is dead.'

'I know it,' I said.

'He kilt in the fire,' the other said. 'A big beam fall on him.'

'Did you see it?' I asked. 'Were you there?'

The taller boy squatted down on the grass, rubbing his hands together for warmth. 'My auntie say your pappy set that fire hisself and shot hisself in the head, so he dead already when the beam came down on him.'

'You're a liar,' I said.

'That's what my auntie say,' he replied, keeping his eyes on his friend, who nodded his head in agreement.

It was a lie, of course. It was not possible that Father would do such a thing. It was an outrage that they should seek me out to tell me this lie which they had made up just to hurt me. My sadness and confusion turned to rage. I wanted to kill the boys and they seemed to know they should be afraid of me, for when I said, 'You'd better run,' they took off like scared rabbits and didn't stop until they were out of sight behind the house. I stood on the dock, shaking with fury.

It started to rain, but I couldn't move. I just stood there until I was soaked through and my teeth were chattering and then I stood there until it was getting dark and Celeste came out and found me. By the time we got back to the house, I was delirious with fever.

I never told anyone this lie the boys told me. Perhaps it

51

never happened and I only dreamed it when I was sick. The doctor and my uncle agreed that Father's death was an accident. Mother always said he'd been murdered. They never did find out how the fire started.

Lies, I thought, lies without end. We lived on them, all of us, all the time.

The image of Sarah as I had seen her leaving my husband's room filled my head, banishing these unendurable recollections. Her hair was all undone, her eyes bright, she was wearing a loose dressing gown I'd never seen before and a dark mantle pulled over it. I had only the quickest look at her in the lamplight, but I'd seen a great deal. And so had the doctor, I didn't doubt, when he opened his door and spoke to her. What had he said? My head began to hammer. The room was so hot I was suffocating. I staggered to the dresser and poured out a glass of water, drank half of it, then poured the rest down the front of my shift. It was as if someone had slapped me. In the distance I could hear shouting, the tolling of the bell. I gripped the table and hung my head forward, trembling from head to foot. A feeling of dread crept over me as I realized that I was laughing.

~

All night I prayed myself a widow, but to prove there is no Supreme Being who hears our prayers, in the morning Sarah came to my door with the message that my husband had gone to his brother's house and would not return until dinner. He wants to borrow more money, I thought, and he will be in a foul humor when he returns. 'Has the doctor gone as well?' I asked.

'Yes, missus,' she said.

'Then I won't go down. Just bring me bread and coffee and a little Creole cheese.'

'Yes, missus,' she said again and went out.

I fell back among the pillows and closed my eyes against the racket of my thoughts. Through it, I could hear the same scratching in the wall I noticed last night: a mouse or squirrel doing no end of damage. Good, I thought. Eat a little every day until it all falls down around our ears. I heard Sarah on the stairs and roused myself. I was washing my face at the stand when she came in with the tray. 'Is the mill burned to the ground?' I asked, bathing my face with my hands.

She put the tray on the side table and stood with her back to me. 'I don' know,' she said.

I patted my face with the hand towel, studying her back. Did she know I saw her last night, leaving his room? 'I hate it when you pretend to be stupid,' I said.

This appealed to her vanity, which is immense. 'They put it out,' she said. 'Only the roof was half-burned and the rest fell in from the water.'

'Too bad,' I said, leaving her to guess if I'd hoped for more or less of our ruin.

I sat at the dressing table, touching the dark circles beneath my eyes while she poured out the coffee and brought it to me. As she leaned across me to place the brimming cup in the only space clear of bottles or pins, her reflection obscured my own. Her eyes were lowered, her hand steady, a single line of concentration on her brow all that gave evidence of any feeling about what she was doing. A very different look from the one I'd seen in the night as she rushed from my husband's bedroom. A flood of anger rose in me, right up to my throat, so that I gasped for air. In panic, I raised my hand, and as I did I knocked her arm. The cup tipped out of the saucer, splattering coffee across the dresser. I leaped away to keep it from running onto my gown. 'Why are you so clumsy?' I exclaimed. Sarah grabbed the hand towel and began mopping up the mess. I went to the window. It was already hot; the sky was the color of lead. 'I can't stand much more,' I said.

~

According to my husband, the conflagration at the mill only proves that he is a flawless manager, far more intelligent and efficient than my father, who might be alive today if he'd had the benefit of his son-in-law's advice.

The fire was started by a man who had been whipped for being too slow in the field. He told two of his fellows of his plan and they informed Cato, the driver, who made it his business to know at every moment the whereabouts of the malcontent. Late last night, when Cato learned the plotter had not been seen in the quarter since supper, he followed the procedure my husband had given him. He ran to Mr Sutter's house and bid him come to the mill at once. He then dispatched two men to alert my husband and another to ring the bell, summoning all hands to the scene. The culprit had managed to pull a few bales of hay inside the mill, douse them with kerosene and light the blaze, but as he came out the door Mr Sutter ran up with his rifle and shot him. He is now in shackles awaiting justice. The bucket line, swiftly organized, proceeded to extinguish the flames. The roof was not a great loss, my husband maintains, as it had needed repairs. Indeed, the lumber is already cut.

'Then everything is as it should be,' I observed.

'I wish that were true,' he said, with a glance at Sarah that meant he could not convey some news of great import before a witness. This irritated me. 'Come to my office when you have finished eating,' he said seriously. 'I must speak to you in private.'

'As you wish,' I said. When he was gone, I dawdled over my coffee. Sarah cleared his place and went out, leaving me alone. The room was quiet, but not for long. No sooner had I taken a deep breath than I blew it out in a huff at the grotesque babbling and clatter just beyond the doors. It was Walter, set loose on the lawn. There is never a moment's peace in this house, I thought. Then I got up and went to hear my husband's report from the outside world.

As soon as I was inside his office, he bade me close the door. He was in an agitated state, unable to sit down. He insisted that I be seated as I would not be able to stand before the ghastly news he had to relate. I was weary from lack of sleep and in no mood for his self-important fantasies, but there was something odd about him, something new that interested me. Of course he looked haggard; he'd spent the night fighting the fire and the morning on horseback, but it wasn't fatigue that had put such hectic color in his cheeks and a queer darting light in his eye. I took my chair willingly enough and gave my attention to his story.

Near dawn, when he was returning to the house, having extinguished the fire and much relieved that it had not altered his fortunes, a boy he recognized as belonging to his brother Charles rode up with an urgent summons. He was entreated to come at once to Charles's plantation, Chatterly, and to bring Dr Landry if he was still on our property. My husband and the doctor rode out together, arriving in time to find the family at breakfast, but an anxious and hurried meal it was. Maybelle, my sister-in-law, was prostrate from terror and exhaustion, their daughters were packing to leave for the safety of New Orleans; their son, Edmund, a boy of fifteen, had persuaded his father to let him stay.

The day before, three runaways had broken into the larder at Chatterly. They had canvas sacks, which they filled with whatever they could carry. The cook, spying them from the kitchen window, raised the alarm. Charles happened to be in the yard, speaking to the farrier. He took up his pistol and came running, arriving in time to wound one of the men, though not seriously enough to prevent their escape. They made for the woods, where, in spite of heated pursuit by hounds and horses, they were not to be found. It was as if the forest had swallowed them up.

Late last night, at perhaps the very hour our mill went up in flames (my husband assumed his most ponderous tone to remind me of this coincidence), a stableboy, walking back to the quarter at Chatterly, was assaulted by two of these men brandishing machetes. They beat him, then hacked off both his arms and legs, leaving him to die. 'Tell your master we done this because he shot one of our men,' they told him. The unfortunate boy lived only long enough to deliver this message to the overseer.

'What are we to do?' my husband concluded. 'Open our larders to every runaway who is tired of working so that those who are faithful will not be murdered? What can they possibly imagine will be the result of such unconscionable savagery?'

I made no response. Indeed the story had shocked me, and I found myself calculating the amount of time it would take a man to walk from my brother-in-law's plantation to this one.

'Suppose it had been Edmund?' my husband speculated. 'That is what has put poor Maybelle under the doctor's care.'

'What *will* you do?' I asked.

'Of course, we'll raise a patrol and apprehend them,' he said. 'It's damned bad timing. Between hauling timber and the mill repairs I'm shorthanded, but I've no choice.'

'But if the dogs failed to find them before . . . ?'

He stopped before me, stroking his mustache, his eyes narrowed. He was trying to decide whether to tell me something more. 'They found a structure in a tree,' he said. 'A house of sorts, with all sorts of comforts, a washstand, a mattress, a tin of tobacco, there was even a deck of cards.'

'Then they have been there for some time.'

'The sheriff has estimated there may be as many as one hundred.'

'Surely that is an exaggerated figure!' I exclaimed.

He left off worrying his mustache and looked at me thoughtfully. 'We can only hope you are right,' he said.

~

In spite of the elaborate secrecy with which the planters will veil their scheme to avenge this crime at Chatterly, there can be little doubt that the negroes there will know everything about it before they ride out, and that these runaways will be informed. Else why would they have taken such a risk and warned the very people they plan to rob of their intention to rob them? My husband marvels at their savagery; I am more astounded by their boldness. It must be their intention to lure their enemies into their neighborhood, where they have somehow learned to survive, even to flourish, and then to cut them down. The woods abutting Chatterly are on low, swampy ground; the undergrowth is impenetrable, full of snakes, thorn bushes, and all manner of stinging insects. Even with oxen it is difficult to haul out much timber, as Charles never stops pointing out, though it's much the same here. In such a place a man on horseback must be an easy target for a man who has contrived to live in a tree.

These were my thoughts in the afternoon as I sat in my room at my sewing. They filled me with trepidation, for we are outnumbered here, as everywhere along the river, and when the planters band together on a hunt, their houses and relations are left undefended. But there was also the thin, scarcely voiced hope that my husband might go out and never return. I had set Sarah to ripping an old gown for quilting, and the repetitive whine of the tearing silk punctuated my musings. Her baby made small congested sounds in its crate. I could see its dark hand moving against the slats. She sat with her back to it, methodically tearing the cloth, absorbed in the task, or so it seemed. I wondered how much she knew about my husband's urgent errand. Did she share my timid wish that it might put her master in danger? I could not ask this question, yet I had a desire to hear her speak. 'What did the doctor say about Walter?' I said.

She glanced up at me, then back to her work, her expression as blank as a death mask. 'He don' hear.'

'Did he make any recommendations for treatment?'

'All master say is he don' hear.'

'Does that one hear?' I asked, gesturing to the baby. For answer, Sarah laid the cloth in her lap, turned toward the creature, and clapped her palms together, making a sharp crack, like a shot. The baby's hands flew up above the top of the box and it let out a soft cry of surprise. Sarah turned back to her work, her mouth set in an annoying smirk.

'Why not just answer me?' I protested. She had come to the hem of the gown, which she pulled free of the skirt in one long shriek.

~

Later, when my husband came upstairs, I heard his footsteps stop before my door. He had drunk wine and brandy at supper, as he often does when the prospect of murdering negroes is before him. I lay still, staring at the doorknob, but it did not turn and presently he went on to his own room.

When Walter was born, I lost what little desire I had for my husband. I knew he was driven to my bed because he feared he had fathered the only son he would ever have. I was nearly blind with resentment and could only get through the ordeal of our conjugal encounters by recourse to a steadily waning sense of duty. I've no doubt my repugnance showed. I was too proud to beg for my freedom, my husband too absorbed in his own passion to notice my suffering. My revulsion turned to resistance and I discovered that this inflamed him further, that it could be useful as a means of bringing the unpleasant process to a speedy conclusion. And so I practiced a mock resistance. Afterward I wept with frustration while my panting husband collapsed at my side. 'Don't cry,' he said, patting my shoulder as he drifted off to sleep. 'We will have a child. I'm sure of it.'

It was not long after my consultation with Dr Sanchez that I found the means to make my husband quit my bed. Indeed, Dr Sanchez unwittingly provided it – it was the sleeping tincture. I found that if I drank two glasses of port at supper and took two spoons of this excellent medicine before getting into bed, I was so perfectly indifferent to my husband that I could endure his embraces without feeling anything at all. I offered neither encouragement nor resistance; I was there and not there at the same time. This frustrated him beyond endurance. He pushed and pulled at me, repeated my name, all to no avail. One night, after only a few weeks of this campaign, he pulled me up roughly by my arms and slapped me hard across the face. I smiled and fell back on the pillow, tasting blood. I brought my fingers to my lips, smearing a little of the blood across my cheek. Abruptly he pulled away from me and sat on the edge of the bed, rubbing his face between his hands. 'Manon,' he said. 'What are you doing?'

'Are you finished already?' I asked agreeably.

'I've not much interest in making love to a corpse,' he said.

I laughed. How wonderful that he would call what we were doing 'making love,' how amusing that he drew the line at a corpse. 'If I am dead,' I said, 'it is because you have killed me.'

He turned to look at me. To my surprise there were tears standing in his eyes. 'The doctor is right,' he said. 'You are unbalanced.'

'Is that his diagnosis?' I said.

He turned away, bending to the floor to pull on his trousers.

Unbalanced, I thought. So that was the name they had for a woman who could not pretend a villain was as good as a decent man. I closed my eyes and opened them again against a wave of nausea. The doctor was right; the balance was not perfect. A little less port in the mix, and maybe a few more drops of the tincture. 'I don't care,' I said as my husband took up his boots and went to the door.

He looked back at me, confounded.

'I don't care what you do,' I said. 'I don't care what you think. I just want you to leave me alone.'

'So be it,' he said, and went out.

There is cholera and yellow fever in New Orleans. We have heard rumors of it, but Dr Landry, stopping here this morning to rest his horse on his way to the city, gave us an alarming confirmation. In the last weeks the cases have been multiplying rapidly, hundreds are already dead, and he does not doubt that a full epidemic is under way. The yellow fever is more dangerous to those who have not long resided in the area – the Americans are particularly prone to contract it – but cholera respects no barriers and even carries away the negroes, who are immune to many diseases that attack the more delicate constitution of the Creole. He bade me bring my mother out of town.

My husband made a thoughtful face at this suggestion, dissembling his real feelings. Mother's rare visits to this house have met with little success. She gives my husband unsolicited advice about farm matters, even criticizing his management of the livestock. Her servant, Peek, doesn't get on with Delphine, and there is a good deal of sullenness in the kitchen. Worst of all for him, I've no doubt, is the necessity to hide the true state of his relations with Sarah. When Walter was a baby and easily banished to the quarter, it was easier, but even then he was forced to curb his temper and his eye when Sarah was about. Mother repeatedly remarks that it is uncommon to have a woman serve at table; why do we not have a proper butler? I enjoy his discomfiture, but unfortunately Mother's criticism extends to my conduct as well. She encourages me to show more warmth to my husband, even if I do not feel it, as it is my duty and, with practice, must become my pleasure. She repeatedly cites the tiresome adage about flies, honey, and vinegar, as if it contains the wisdom of the ages.

'I will send for her at once,' I told Dr Landry, and all my husband could do was nod agreement. When they had gone, I went straight to the desk and wrote the invitation. But no sooner had I finished writing and stood fanning the page than there was a clatter on the drive. A barefoot mulatto boy came running into the hall, breathless from terror. He said he had been stopped three times on the road by the patrols, who demanded his pass and quizzed him closely on his business. Fortunately my mother's doctor had written 'Urgent' on the letter he was carrying and stamped both the envelope and the pass with his seal; otherwise, the boy exclaimed, he would have been shot off his master's horse.

I took the letter; a chill ran along my spine at the feel of it, and I sent the child to the kitchen to be fed and comforted by Delphine. I broke the seal and took out the single sheet of vellum.

'Dear Manon,' the letter read. 'I'm sorry to inform you that your mother is badly taken. I fear she will not last more than a day or two. She has asked me to send for you. You'd best leave at once. Sincerely, J. Chapin, M.D.'

My husband came in as I stood rereading this brief message. I couldn't remember Mother ever being seriously ill one day in her life. 'It's from Mother's doctor,' I said to his questioning look. 'He says she is dying.'

'Is it the cholera?' he asked.

'He doesn't say,' I replied.

Fake sympathy muddled his expression. I saw through it his deep calculation, to which I dealt a sure and devastating blow. 'I'll be off as soon as I can pack,' I said, walking toward the stairs. Then, as if it were an afterthought, I added over my shoulder, 'I'll take Sarah with me.'

PART TWO

~

En Ville

Nothing could have been more laughable than the touching scene of our departure: the master bids farewell to his wife and servant, tremulous with the fear that one of them may not return. But which one? He wishes I might die of cholera, and fears that she may instead. I wish he might be killed while shooting rebellious negroes. She wishes us both dead. He actually had tears standing in his eyes. He took my hands and poured upon me a look of tender solicitude. 'Write to let me know that you have arrived safely,' he said. Rose came in carrying Sarah's baby, a sight that dried up his tears fast enough. The poor creature becomes uglier every day, and its hair has come in thick, curly, and red. Sarah took it up and rested it against her shoulder, patting its back absently. 'What could happen to us?' I said.

'I'm not sure whether you will be safer there or here,' he said. 'That is the intolerable state we've come to.' He looked out at the waiting carriage. For a moment I almost pitied him. He is so bound by the lies he tells himself; he can only play at feelings he thinks he should have. He cast a furtive, wistful look over my head at Sarah, and my pity dissolved in a familiar wave of bitterness. 'We must be off,' I said, signaling to the boy to come in for the trunk. Sarah went ahead, carrying the baby and the small travel case. My husband followed me. As I climbed into the carriage, he put his hand under my elbow to assist me. 'Take care, Manon,' he said. I fixed my blandest smile upon my lips as I settled into the seat, arranging my skirts amid the bustle caused by the trunk being lashed into place, Rose handing up a package of biscuits and ham, the driver bounding to his bench and speaking to his horses, the creaking of leather, the crack of the whip, the jolt and groan of iron on wood as the wheels began to turn and we pulled away. I raised my hand to my husband, who stood on the step waving awkwardly. Walter burst from the bushes and ran toward him, his arms thrashing the air, his red hair like a fire burning up his head. He threw himself at his father's legs, screaming, either from joy or pain, there was no telling, and my husband was forced to lean over the child to keep his balance.

'Perfect,' I said to Sarah, who was watching also, squinting against the sun. 'A perfect picture to remind me of the charms of home.'

～

More carriages were leaving the city than going to it, though we were overtaken by two doctors on horseback. Both

68

assured me that the danger was not so great as the populace feared. 'They exaggerate everything in New Orleans,' Dr Petrie of Donaldsonville assured me. 'It's part of the pleasure of living there.' But at dusk, when we reached town, I knew at once that it was Dr Petrie who had exaggerated. How altered it was, how dark and shuttered the houses, how still the fetid air of the streets. There were torches lit at intervals along the way and a sulfurous smoke had spread like a dirty yellow blanket settling over the buildings. To my horror we passed a wagon laden with dead bodies. They were wrapped in linen sheets and a heavy canvas had been thrown over them, but their feet, bruised blue and swollen, stuck out at the back and sides, as if still seeking one last step upon this world. The driver, an aged, skeletal negro who did not so much as raise his eyes as we passed, could have modeled for death himself. Surely he was not much farther from the grave than his cargo. What if Mother was in that lot? I thought. I closed my eyes and made a vow that if she was not, and if she were to die, I would take her to the cemetery in my own carriage rather than see her carted off in so promiscuous a manner.

Sarah's baby was mewing, then, as her mother tried to comfort her, she gave over to a loud, nerve-racking wail that made me want to pitch her into the street. 'Can't you make her stop?' I said, after a few minutes of this.

'She hungry,' Sarah said, shifting the child to her shoulder. Sarah was wide-eyed, her upper lip damp with perspiration, and she was holding herself in an unnaturally stiff position, her chin pressed in to her neck, her nostrils pinched as if she was having trouble breathing. She's scared to death, I thought. She'll be as much use as a cat when we get there.

At last we turned onto Rue St Ann and pulled up in front of Mother's cottage. It too was shuttered; I had rarely seen it closed up so entirely. I leaped from the carriage, ran up the few steps, and yanked impatiently on the cord. I could hear the bell clanging in the back of the house, then silence. For a moment I feared I was ringing a bell inside a tomb, then, to my relief, I heard footsteps coming toward the door.

It was Peek, Mother's cook. She opened the inner door hesitantly, then, seeing me through the shutter, pulled the latch and floor bolt to let me in. Sarah had climbed down and stood beside me, her baby fretting against her shoulder. 'Miss Manon,' Peek said. 'Your mama is a little better today.'

'Go straight back and quiet that child,' I told Sarah. 'All a sick person needs is a whining baby in the house.' I went into the parlor. How dreary and dark it was, and how still. Sarah continued out through the dining room to the quarter. Peek stood on the step waiting for the driver to unfasten my trunk. My eyes fell upon a framed portrait of Father on the side table. He'd had it made for Mother when they were first married. He said the artist had romanticized him; that his hair had never been so thick, his jaw so prominent, but Mother maintained it was a good likeness. 'I wish you were here,' I said. 'I miss you so.' Then I went through the dining room to Mother's bedroom door.

~

Mother is not an easy patient, and I am certainly not constituted to enjoy nursing duties. She is too weak to stand,
petulant and weepy, unable to hold down anything but clear
broth. Dr Chapin has visited regularly and yesterday
pronounced her to be improving, but he confided to me as
we left the room that it is not uncommon in this disease for
a patient to rally for a few days and then to be taken off
suddenly. Her own view is that the doctor is killing her.
Indeed, his treatment is bleeding and laxatives, which, to
be effective, he insists must be administered at frequent
intervals. As Mother's fever has broken, he has relented,
and the result has been a gradual strengthening of our
patient. 'Keep him away from me,' Mother says every time
the bell rings. She prefers Peek's poultices and teas, which
smell strong enough to drive a devil from the room.

I look forward to the doctor's visits if Mother does not.
He brings news from outside the cottage. The yellow fever
is generally lessening, having, as he puts it, lost its hold
on the population. The cholera has carried off over one
hundred people this week, many of them negroes, at great
expense to the community. The graveyards are over-
flowing; there are not enough gravediggers to keep up
with the demand. No one goes out but to obtain food,
there are no parties, no public gatherings of any kind. The
city is as it might be under enemy siege. Yet, as the days
slip by, I am strangely at peace. I sleep in my old room
at the front of the house, and take my meals alone in the
courtyard.

Mother bought this cottage after Father died, to be close
to her own mother, who was infirm. I was thirteen when

71

we moved here. When I first saw it, I thought it would be too small for comfort or privacy; there are only four rooms in the front house, two on the street, two behind, but they are large, airy, and so designed that each can be closed off from the others. From the dining room two sets of casements open on to the courtyard, which is half covered by a gallery running between the kitchen and the two-room quarter. This creates a comfortable covered loggia which is always cool. There is a lovely old marble column dividing this space between two graceful arches, and beyond it a pool fed from the cistern. I sew there in the afternoons, and I can hear Mother's bell should she wake from her nap. Sarah sits on the kitchen step peeling vegetables or skimming one of Peek's noxious medicinal brews. She's found a rocking cradle somewhere which she works with her foot. Even the steady creak of this device does not disturb me; in fact, it has a soothing effect, as if I were being rocked to sleep myself.

Of course it occurs to me that should mother relapse and be taken by her illness, this little house would be my own.

~

I have been through a living nightmare.

At noon I went in to feed Mother some broth. She seemed much improved. She asked to be settled in her chair and was strong enough to get there by holding on to my arm and taking small steps. She wanted various pillows arranged just so, then complained that the soup was not hot, which made me think of my husband. I called Sarah to take it to the kitchen and put it back on the fire. When Sarah came in, Mother gave her a long look, as if she could not think who she was. Then, when she had gone out, Mother said to me, 'Why have you brought that one with you?'

'Why shouldn't I? She's mine,' I said.

'But who is serving your husband?'

'Rose, I imagine. She's old enough. I left in such a hurry that was the last thing on my mind.'

'So you still have no proper butler,' Mother said.

'My husband does not wish to have one.'

She was silent a moment, studying me in a way that made me uncomfortable. 'Can't he afford one?' she asked.

'I don't know,' I lied. 'I'm not privy to his finances.'

'Why did he choose sugar?' she fretted, more to herself than to me. 'There's no reliable profit in it.'

'No,' I agreed. 'Cotton is more practical.'

'I keep hearing a baby crying,' she said abruptly. 'Is there a baby here?'

'It's Sarah's,' I said. 'She's still suckling.'

'Why did you bring her here?' she asked again. Her persistence perplexed me, so I gave no answer. Her mind is wandering, I thought, from her illness.

'Whose baby is it?' she asked again.

'Sarah's,' I said.

'Yes,' she said impatiently. 'I know that. But who is the father?'

'How should I know?' I said. She blinked at me, as if I'd struck her.

'I thought you would manage better than you have,

73

Manon,' she said. 'You neglect your duties and so you have no control in your own house.'

I could not bear another lecture on my failings as a wife. 'How long can it take to warm a bowl of soup?' I said, rising from my seat. Just as I reached the door, Sarah appeared with the tray. 'At last,' I said. 'What makes you so slow?' I reached out to take the tray, but as I did so I saw that Sarah was looking past me with a grimace of revulsion. She backed away, allowing the tray to slip from her fingers and crash to the floor. Hot soup flew up onto my skirt; a few drops burned my ankles. I shouted, turning away to pull a towel from the washstand, and, as I did, I saw a sight so terrible it will haunt my dreams until I die. Mother was sitting just as she had been, propped on her pillows, her hands folded in her lap, but from her mouth, nose, eyes, and ears, a black fluid gushed forth. I screamed. Sarah ran, calling for Peek. I took up a towel and went to Mother, pressing it to her mouth and nose. She didn't struggle. Perhaps she was already dead. 'My God,' I said, over and over, mopping the viscous fluid away, but to no avail. I took her hand to find even her fingernails blackened and wet, and when I looked down, I saw two stains unfurling like black flowers at the toes of her linen slippers. 'Can you hear me?' I said, as the towel turned slippery in my hands. Peek came running in, trailing towels, went straight to the washstand, filled the bowl, and brought it to me. Together we washed Mother's face and neck as best we could. Soon the water in the bowl was black, and still the liquid seeped from her eyes and mouth. Her skin had turned blue, as if she were suffocating, and the veins in

74

her neck and hands stood out against the flesh like spreading black tentacles. 'Mother,' I pleaded. 'Please speak to me. Please try to speak to me.' Peek put her hand on my arm and said, 'She gone, missus. Nothing more you can do.'

My legs gave out beneath me and I dropped to my hands and knees on the carpet. 'Mother,' I said. A loose strand of my hair fell across my cheek. The tip of it was black and so wet that a thick drop landed on my splayed fingers. There was someone else in the room, I knew. Someone had come in. I looked up to see Sarah, squatting near the door, picking up the broken china and placing the pieces on the tray. 'Leave it,' I said. 'Leave me.' She lifted her head to look at me; we were level there on the floor. She was biting her lower lip with her upper teeth, looking down her nose at me, I thought, with about as much sympathy as a lizard. Behind me I could hear Peek weeping. Sarah stood up and backed out the door.

'Help me up,' I said to Peek.

~

Peek and I washed Mother's body, dressed her in a clean linen gown, and laid her flat upon her bed. Her face was swollen, of a brickish hue, her eyes bulging, the whites as yellow as a lemon's flesh. We tried to close her eyes, to cover the black line between her lips with powder, but our efforts proved futile. I couldn't bear to see her so disfigured. At last I put a pillowcase over her head and left the room.

I sent off two letters, one to my aunt and one to my husband, informing them of Mother's sudden death. My aunt was staying at her summer house near the lake, so I thought to hear from her before the morning. I ate only a little soup and bread, then called Sarah to sit in the court with me and help sew together two sheets for a shroud. Peek was burning a bit of horseskin and a hoof, which is said to ward off the infectious vapors of one who has succumbed. It filled the air with an odor bad enough to punish the living for having survived. Peek, who is usually talkative, was quiet, tending her fire with a stick, occasionally wiping a tear from her eyes. She's afraid to ask what will become of her, I thought, and I couldn't tell her if she did ask, as I don't know what is in Mother's will.

We finished our work as the daylight faded. I had Sarah light the lamps in the parlor and went inside. I was certain I would not sleep, as I had forgotten my tincture in the rush to depart. I couldn't bear the thought of lying awake in my room. But what was I to do? I was tired of sewing, my thoughts too agitated even to read a journal, it did not seem proper to play the old piano, which was probably out of tune. I went to Mother's desk with some notion of organizing her papers, though she was the most orderly person I have ever known and I doubted I would find anything amiss. I heard Sarah's baby screaming from the kitchen. 'Bring me a glass of port,' I told Sarah, 'and then get that child and come sit in here. I'm expecting a letter from my aunt and I want you to answer the bell.'

She filled a glass at the sideboard and brought it to me. I opened a drawer and took out Mother's account book.

Sarah stood next to me, watching my hands as I turned the pages. 'What is it?' I said, but she made no reply and went out. I ran my finger down the column of numbers in the margin.

After Father died, Mother sold the farm and most of the slaves, used part of the profit to buy her house, and invested the rest to create a small income. She kept track of every penny. I saw at once that she had been living well inside that income and had, in fact, been steadily increasing the capital over the years. If my husband gets his hands on this money, I thought, it will be gone in a month. I recalled Sally Pemberly, who had managed to rescue her dowry from her husband's extravagance, and resolved to learn the name of her lawyer.

In a side drawer I found three packets of letters neatly tied with black ribbon. Two were from my mother's brother, the third was from my grandmother. At the back was what appeared at first to be another, older account book. The edges were frayed, the brown leather cover much faded. As I opened it, Sarah came in with her baby and sat on the settee near the door. The child was whining softly, but as soon as her mother had opened her dress she grew quiet, occasionally making lip-smacking sounds, like a man savoring his meat. With a thrill, I recognized my father's handwriting, page after page of it, closely written, the entries dated. It was a diary, started just two years before he died. What a treasure, I thought, but I had no moment to read even one sentence before the bell rang and Sarah leaped up, detaching the baby from her breast and buttoning her bodice as she went to the door. I closed the diary, thinking to examine it at some quieter time. Sarah came back in, followed by a boy I recognized as one of ours. 'He means to stay the night here,' she said. 'It's too late for him to go back.'

'Has he a pass?' I asked.

The boy produced a strip of pasteboard from his pocket and held it out to me. 'Master say I should stay,' he said boldly. 'He say Mistress send a letter by me in the morning.'

'I've already written to him,' I said. 'Our letters have crossed.'

The boy hung his head, casting a stealthy look about the room at the same time.

'Very well,' I said, breaking the seal of the letter. 'You may stay.'

'Yes, missus,' he said.

I rang for Peek, who came in covered with flour. 'This boy is to stay here tonight,' I said.

'Where he to sleep?' Peek said, eyeing the child. 'The kitchen table?'

'Just make a place for him,' I said, extracting the single sheet from the envelope. As the boy followed Peek back to her domain, I moved close to the lamp to read my husband's cramped handwriting. If only I'd had an example of his epistolary style before I agreed to marry him. But he had been careful to send the briefest messages, apprising me only of his expected arrivals and departures in town. Stupidly I took his terseness as proof that he was a man of affairs, but now I know it is because he is so dull he can think of but few words to say. This missive, though brief, was unusually expansive and informative.

My dear Manon,

I write to tell you of events after your departure. As we discussed, I joined the patrol at Chatterly. We routed 15 negroes from the swamp. 10 are dead, 5 awaiting sentencing. The leader was a devilish mulatto from Plaquemines who had escaped from his master four years ago. None of our party are seriously injured, but I am sorry to report that I took a fall from my horse and my ankle was badly sprained. I am slowly recovering.

I trust you arrived safely in town and I pray that your mother's health has improved. We receive such worrisome reports. I will expect word from you by this messenger and look forward to your earliest return.

With loving affection,

His signature, as always, was his initials scrawled together to make both completely illegible.

I laid the letter across Father's journal, then pushed it aside, so strong was my sense that one should not touch the other. I rested my head in my hands. My brain was suddenly raging, my chest tight, my face hot. Everything about the letter appalled me: the condescending tone, the charmless conceit, the element of command at the end, offset by an absurd pretense of warmth in the salutation and the closing. His letter was a perfect miniature of the monument to falsity he has made of my life. Tears filled my eyes, and I made no effort to stanch them. There was no one to help me. When Mother was alive, I had some vain hope that she might come to understand what I have had to bear and take my part, but now even that was gone. How am I to arrange for her burial? I thought frantically. Why has my aunt not written to tell me what to do? I looked around helplessly, wiping my eyes with my sleeve.

Sarah was there in the shadows, watching me. Her bodice was open, her breast exposed. The baby lay still in her lap, breathing peacefully, its dark mouth open to reveal a flat pink tongue. She had rested her head against the back of the settee and her eyes were lowered, her shoulders relaxed. The flickering light from the lamp bronzed her skin and made her eyes glisten like wet black stones. She was enormously still.

I wiped the last of my tears away as I looked at her, my head awash in pain. Why did he let her keep that child? I thought. What had she done to make him agree to it, what bargain had she struck, what promise given?

And then, as if to answer me, a white drop formed at her nipple and clung there. She made no move to wipe it away, indeed she seemed unaware of it. Her eyes closed, then she looked back at me steadily.

It was for his own pleasure, I thought.

The room was stifling, the air so heavy it seemed to clog my nostrils. I fancied I could smell the decay taking place in Mother's body there in her bedroom, though Peek and I had bathed her with scent only a few hours before. When I stood up, everything whirled around me so that I clutched the chair. *We receive such worrisome reports,* I thought, and I could hear my husband's nasal voice. I steadied myself and took a few steps toward the shadows where Sarah sat. 'Put the child by,' I said.

She leaned forward, lifting the sleeping creature by its shoulders and sliding it onto the cushion next to her, where it made the slightest murmur, moved its thumb to its mouth, and drifted back into sleep. *I am sorry to report.* My husband's world was full of reports. He'd managed to use the word twice in a letter of ten lines. I pictured him, limping across the dining room on his bad ankle. When we got back, he'd use Sarah for support. If he were dead, I thought, my heart aching in my chest.

Sarah was sitting forward, her long hands folded in her lap, her eyes resting on the child. The drop of milk still clung to the dark flesh of her nipple; it seemed a wonder to me that it should. I dropped to my knees on the carpet before her and rested my hands upon her wrists. I could feel the smooth, round bones through the thin cloth of her sleeve. I leaned forward until my mouth was close to her breast, then put out my tongue to capture the drop.

It dissolved instantly, leaving only a trace of sweetness. I raised my hand, cupping her breast, which was lighter than I would have thought. It seemed to slip away from my fingers, but I guided the nipple to my lips and sucked gently. Nothing happened. I took it more deeply into my mouth and sucked from my cheeks. This is what he does, I thought. At once a sharp, warm jet hit my throat and I swallowed to keep from choking. How thin it was, how sweet! A sensation of utter strangeness came over me, and I struggled not to swoon. I could see myself, kneeling there, and beyond me the room where my mother's body lay, yet it seemed to me she was not dead, that she bore horrified witness to my action. And beyond that I could see my husband in his office, lifting his head from his books with an uncomfortable suspicion that something important was not adding up. This vision made me smile. I closed my eyes, swallowing greedily. I was aware of a sound, a sigh, but I was not sure if it came from me or from Sarah. How wonderful I felt, how entirely free. My headache disappeared, my chest seemed to expand, there was a complementary tingling in my own breasts. I opened my eyes and looked at Sarah's profile. She had lifted her chin as far away from me as she could, her mouth was set in a thin, hard line, and her eyes were focused intently on the arm of the settee. She's afraid to look at me, I thought. And she's right to be. If she looked at me, I would slap her.

The bell sounded so harshly we both leaped to our feet. I turned to the desk, wiping my mouth against my hand. Sarah hastily fastened her dress and went to the door, glancing back only to see that her baby was secure on its cushion. I heard the bolts pulled, the creaking of the shutter hinges, and then my aunt's voice, coming toward me. 'My poor darling,' she said, as I went to her and she embraced me. 'What a frightful time you must have had. Look, you are as white as a sheet. I came the moment I received your message.'

~

In a town where half the population is dead and the other half in hourly terror of dying, it is no easy matter to arrange a decent funeral. Mercifully my aunt set herself to the task at once. She sent an announcement to the newspaper, ordered the casket and a private hearse, and notified the cemetery of the proposed ceremony. I would have preferred to bury Mother in St Francisville with Father and my two baby brothers, but there was no time, nor place for her there, so she must be laid to rest in the Petrie crypt with her mother and grandparents on her mother's side. My aunt and I made a list of Mother's relations and friends. While she went out to engage the priest, I sent cards to these people. I added Joel Borden's name, because he was so kind to Mother and she so fond of him. I doubted that he was in town, but I wanted him to be notified upon his return.

We had just finished dinner when a second letter arrived from my husband. It was in his formal style, as if he'd recently made my acquaintance, and referred to my mother as Mrs Gray. I read, with relief, that he was unable to attend the funeral because of his recent injury and the pressing necessity of the repairs to the mill. How far away, how long ago, my life with him seemed as I read aloud his expressions of regret and sympathy to my aunt.

'It's just as well,' she observed. 'We don't need anyone else being carried off by this pestilence. As soon as my poor sister is buried, we should all leave town until the weather turns.'

But I had no wish to leave.

Toward dusk my aunt and I went into Mother's room to place her body in the shroud. My aunt pressed my arm and said solemnly, 'Manon, I have seen how this disease disfigures its victims. I pray you will understand when I say I would rather not see my sister's face.'

'I can't wish anyone who cared for her to share the

memory I have,' I said truthfully, and she touched my cheek in sympathy. We left the pillowcase covering Mother's face, slipped the shroud over her body, and stitched it closed at her feet.

We sat in the parlor sewing until it was dark. I was so exhausted I continually spoiled my work, ripping out as many stitches as I put in. My aunt, observing my frustration, urged me to bed. As I passed through the dining room I heard Peek and Sarah talking softly in the court. Peek was still weeping; there was a tearful catch in her voice. Unless Mother made some other plan for her, I thought, she is mine now. Sarah was doubtless telling her how hard her life will be when she comes to the country. In truth I hate to bring her there because she won't get on with Delphine, though they are much alike. We have no need for a contrary cook. 'Another mouth to feed,' I said as I collapsed across the bed, straight into a dreamless sleep.

~

The foul vapors of the sickroom were inadequate preparation for the pestilential stench of the cemetery, yet at the gates we were accosted by free negroes who had set up as purveyors of meat pies and orgeat water. My aunt and I exchanged incredulous looks, pressing our handkerchiefs to our noses beneath our veils, as our carriage followed the hearse into what seemed to me the very vestibule of hell. Everywhere we looked, rough pine coffins were scattered in groups, awaiting gravediggers. Some had broken open in the drop from the cart, exposing their contents to great swarms of flies. I saw one box, tipped on its side, from which a shock of long black hair poured out into the mud. At every crossing there were pyramids of bones, dug out and stacked to make room for the new arrivals. The gravediggers, crude Irishmen cursing the dead, plied their shovels in knee-deep water. With a gasp my aunt pointed to a mourning couple, the woman hiding her face in the man's arms, while he looked on tearfully at two negroes who stood on either end of a floating coffin endeavoring to seesaw it into the watery grave. How grateful I was that Mother's family owned a crypt. My grandfather had purchased it after a spring flood sent coffins floating down the streets of the Carré. In our city, as my uncle says, underground means underwater.

The scene at this edifice was hardly less grisly. There had been a general winnowing of the dead in the crypts and the bones had simply been tossed onto the path, so we were forced to alight from the carriage with care that our skirts not sweep some finger or thighbone along with us. To our relief, Père François had arrived, the crypt was open, and three negroes stood ready to move Mother's coffin into place. My aunt, weakened by the sun and sickened by the atmosphere, clung to my arm as we approached. The priest came quickly to her aid, murmuring his condolences to me even as he signaled the men to unload the hearse. I could not speak. I thought of how little Mother had liked Père François, of Father's skepticism about what he called 'your mother's superstition.' The negroes labored past us, shouldering the coffin, shoved it into the space with much groaning and sweating, and backed away, their foreman being careful to pass close enough to my aunt to receive the carefully folded bill she extracted from her sleeve. The priest droned some prayers in Latin, made the sign of the cross, which my aunt and I copied like monkeys, and we were done, all of us eager to get far away from the place as fast as we could, lest we inhale that which might keep us there forever. Once we were seated in the carriage, I closed my eyes and kept them closed until I felt the horses pick up their step at the gate.

Great billows of dark clouds were rolling in from the north, and there were flashes of lightning followed by low and distant thunder. In the short time it took to get back to the town, the sun was obscured, the temperature dropped notably, and a few drops spattered against the sill. My aunt lifted her veil and looked out hopefully. 'Perhaps our prayers will be answered,' she said, which amused me. People are always praying for the weather to change and, as it eventually must, they conclude they have been instrumental in effecting what was actually inevitable. My husband continually urges me to pray for rain or, after it comes, to pray for it to stop.

More and more drops fell. By the time we turned onto Rue St. Ann it was a steady downpour. We pulled up to the curb, where I was annoyed to see the front door wide open and Sarah standing outside under the abat-vent, in casual conversation with a mulatto man I did not recognize. 'Why, it is Mr Roget,' my aunt observed. She drew her skirt around her in preparation for her descent.

'And who is Mr Roget?' I asked, frowning at this person who had the impudence to tip his hat to me before he turned and walked away. Sarah slipped back into the shadows of the doorway.

'He is the fellow who wanted to buy Sarah from your uncle,' she replied. 'He was quite a pest on the subject; still I hated losing him. He is an amiable person and an excellent builder. You should see his faux marble; it's a wonder.' And leaving me with this information, which conveniently omitted my uncle's response to Mr Roget's suit, she called out to the coachman to take her hand, and leaped nimbly across the mud to the banquette.

~

It rained hard all night, and in the morning the air was cool, the sky a pale blue, and the city in a celebratory mood. I looked out the front door to see my neighbors having coffee on their balcony while all around them their house shook with the clatter of shutters being thrown open. Indeed, all up and down the street there was an echoing creak of hinges, the slap of wood against wood, and the occasional call of greeting as neighbors saw one another for the first time in weeks. My aunt came in dressed for church, pulling on her gloves. 'I'm off to mass to give thanks,' she announced cheerfully. 'Won't you join me? Everyone will be there.'

'No, thank you,' I said.

'I don't know how you manage without the consolation of religion.'

'Yet I do,' I said, smiling, having no wish to offend her. Father thought highly of Aunt Lelia and said she could even make a virtue of religion, which was high praise from him.

'Very well, I will pray for you, darling,' she said, coming to kiss my cheek. 'And for your poor mother's soul, which is in heaven.' Sarah came in carrying the breakfast tray. 'In the dining room,' I said, waving her back. I followed my aunt to the door and watched her join a stream of pedestrians at the corner, all elegantly dressed, greeting one another light-heartedly. None, I thought, would name the true cause for his high spirits and say what each one felt: 'Others have died, but I am alive.' I went back into the dining room and took a slice of bread from the plate. I called for Sarah, who appeared in the doorway, her eyes cast down.

She had kept out of my way since the night Mother died, hiding in the kitchen or staying in her hot room with the baby, appearing only when called for. I swallowed the bread, watching her. She seemed to stiffen before my eyes, to become stone, even her eyes didn't blink; it is a trick she has. 'You must know,' I said, 'that servants are not allowed to receive visitors at the front door.'

'Yes, missus,' she said, moving only her lips.

I sat down at the table and tore off another bit of bread. 'Pour me some coffee,' I said. She picked up the pot and leaned over me, directing the hot black stream into my cup. I was certain she knew I knew all about Mr Roget. 'Who was the man you were speaking to yesterday?' I asked.

'His name Mr Roget,' she said. She had a cowed look about her, expecting the worst.

'What was his object in coming here?'

She set the pot carefully on the trivet, then stepped back so that I couldn't see her. 'My brother sent him to tell me he got work on the docks.'

'Who has work? Mr Roget?'

'No, missus. My brother. He hired out from his master to work on the docks.'

'And what is your brother's name?'

'Clarence.'

I sipped my coffee. A brother, I thought. What a clever invention. I wondered if she'd made it up on the spot or if she and Mr Roget had worked it out together. 'It's unusual, isn't it,' I said, 'for a free man to carry messages between two slaves?'

Of course she made no response. After a sufficient silence, I tried of having her standing behind me. 'Leave me,' I said. 'Go and tell Peek to help you open the shutters.'

~

Mother's estate is left entirely to me and is greater than I thought. She had set aside a small inheritance I knew nothing about, and it has grown impressively. So I am to have the house, the furnishings, sufficient income to live comfortably, and two slaves, Peek and a boy named Isaiah whom Mother has hired out to a baker in town. All this is mine, and yet it is not mine, because my husband can, and doubtless will, dispose of it just as soon as I can get it. 'Is there no way to preserve this to myself?' I pleaded with the lawyer.

'Not unless you were to divorce your husband,' he said.

'And that could take years. In the meantime he would have control of the estate.'

My aunt sat beside me, her lips pressed tightly together, trying to block out the word 'divorce' by batting her eyes.

'Of course, when your husband passes away, the property will all come to you,' the lawyer reassured me.

'If there's anything left of it,' I said.

As we left the lawyer's office I observed to my aunt, 'The laws in this state are designed to provoke the citizens to murder.'

She gave me a disapproving look. 'It's the same everywhere,' she said. 'A woman's property is her husband's.'

'My husband won't want Peek. What am I going to do with her?'

'Peek is a problem,' she agreed. 'Come and have coffee with me, and we will discuss it.'

Mother's will requested that Peek should not be sold at market, or hired to any establishment, and that she not be required to leave the city, as, Mother had written, 'she has a terror of country life.'

'I have no wish to keep her,' I told my aunt when we were seated in her drawing room. 'Would you want her for yourself?'

'No,' she said. 'My Ines is an excellent cook. And the unhappy truth is that Peek is not an accomplished chef.'

'Delphine says she can spoil milk just by looking at it,' I said.

My aunt smiled. 'Your poor mother used to borrow Ines for her dinner parties two or three times a month, whenever your uncle and I were dining out.'

'That was generous of you,' I said.

'It was an exchange,' she explained. 'Peek spent the evening in my big kitchen making her medicines for all of us. No one can stand to be in the house when she's at that.'

'Mother swore by her remedies,' I agreed.

'I continually derive benefit from her chest infusion.'

'She does nothing but cry,' I said. 'She thinks I'm going to take her home with me and make her cook for the field hands.'

'That might occasion an insurrection,' my aunt chuckled.

'Do you know how old she is?'

'She wasn't a girl when she came to your mother, and that was twenty years ago. She is fifty or fifty-five, I would guess.'

'She wouldn't bring one hundred dollars at sale.'

'No,' my aunt agreed. 'She has little value.'

We sipped our coffee. I felt at ease, lighthearted, as I seldom do, but as I once did. The furnishings, the paintings, the carpet in my aunt's drawing room all reminded me of happier times. Even the leafy pattern on the saucer in my lap seemed designed especially to please me. 'She should be with someone like Mother,' I concluded. 'A widowed lady, living alone.'

'And one not particular about food,' my aunt added. 'I can't think of anyone in the family.'

'We'll have to find someone to give her to, I suppose,' I said.

'That seems much the best course.'

'Is there someone in the neighborhood?'

After a few moments' thought, my aunt replied, 'I don't

know of anyone. But you might ask Peek. She may have some idea about what to do herself.'

~

And to my surprise, my aunt was right. When I called Peek into the parlor, I was prepared for a scene of tears and lamentation, but as soon as I had related the stipulations of Mother's will, she dried her eyes and showed a keen interest in her fate. 'Miss Favrot will take me to nurse her mother,' she said. 'Her house three blocks from here.'

'How can you be sure?'

'My cousin work in her house. He already spoke for me and his mistress say she take me, but she won't pay no high price.'

'Are you acquainted with this lady?'

'I brought her a remedy for her son one time. He suffer from the croup. He got better when the doctors couldn't do nothin' for him.'

'Very well, Peek,' I said. 'I shall write to this lady today, and you will deliver the letter.' She nodded her head a few times and went out, folding her handkerchief and smoothing her skirt, without so much as a word of thanks.

~

In the evening it was so cool I had a fire in the parlor. I sat at Mother's desk with the intention of examining Father's diary. For the first time I felt myself in possession of the house, an agreeable sensation, unlike any I have ever known. I took out the leather book and opened it to the page on which Father had written the date and his name, printed in large square letters, G. PERCY GRAY. A shiver of pleasure ran along my spine, as if Father were there in the room, though he has been gone these fifteen years.

I turned to the first entry and read an account of the weather, work done in the fields, bills paid; and a brief mention of a visit from a neighbor. This entry covered half the page. The next was similar in style and content. I looked ahead and saw that the entries were all much the same length and addressed the same topics – the weather, the crops, hunting or fishing, infirmities of animals and slaves, money spent, provisions bought – day after day. I was disappointed by the dullness of this record. Father was so full of energy it seemed impossible that he would make no more distinguished account of his life than this list of business and domestic preoccupations. And why had Mother preserved the book, if there was nothing of interest in it? I flipped through the pages, reading at random. News of a fire at a neighbor's gin. *Hands picking poorly, cotton trashy. Three days hard rain, spoiling the bolls.* A visit from the doctor, another from the factor. No mention of Mother or me, as if we didn't exist. A coal sputtered and shot a spark onto the tile. I looked up at the fire, letting the pages fall where they might, and when I looked back again I read this sentence: *Have apologized to my dear wife for my failing, but she says she cannot forgive me now nor ever will.*

For my failing. I read the entry carefully: *May 23. weather fine, unusually chilly in the morning. Scraping cotton this side little creek. Replanting corn. Lice have ruined part of crop, all corn above much eaten. Stopped growing. Dr White here to see my sick ones, seven in number. Old Burns will not recover I fear. Have apologized to my dear wife for my failing, but she says she cannot forgive me now nor ever will.*

The next entry and the next were all concerned with the crops, the weather, a fishing expedition, a trip to the town for jury duty. Another mentioned a dog I scarcely remembered: *my old dog Rattler so crippled, forced to put him down. Where is the God who will put us out of our misery.* I looked ahead, skimming the pages, but found no further mention of this failing. Toward the end there was an entry that concluded, *my dear wife, much vexed, will not forgive me.* This was six months later. The diary filled only half the book. The last entry, made a few days before his death, read: *Cold, damp, sowing oats, number wild geese, burning logs, three with pleurisy, misery in the cabins and the house, rain at dark.*

I closed the book. When Father died, Mother had not forgiven him for something, for some failing, and now I would never know what it was.

After his death, Mother was inconsolable. It was a month before she would speak to anyone but her sister or me. She insisted that the fire was no accident, that Father had been murdered. I slept in her room and heard her every night, calling his name in her sleep. Once I woke to find her standing over my bed, struggling to loosen the high neck of her gown and whispering harshly, 'Percy, Percy,' as if she thought he was strangling her.

I returned the book to the drawer and moved to a chair nearer the fire. There was Father's portrait on the table next to me, a handsome young American, his thick golden hair curling over his smooth brow, a tentative smile on his lips. He had just married a beautiful Creole, much against the wishes of her family, and removed with her to the small farm he had purchased in West Feliciana Parish. He had little money, but he had ambition; he was fearless, godless, principled, and kind. He made a success of his enterprise, not a fortune, but a solid concern, free of debt. What precious little failing was he guilty of that my mother could not find it in her heart to forgive? Did he fail to consult her wishes in every matter that concerned her comfort? Did he fail to tolerate her dependence on a religion that struck him as cruel superstition? Did he fail, perhaps, to bring her some present when he went to the town? How often had I seen him get up from the table to cut her a slice of bread or bring her a cup of coffee, dismissing the servant because, he said, it gave him pleasure to serve her? Did any day go by when he did not compliment her, defer to her, inquire as to her preference or opinion? How was it possible that she should have let him live one hour with the certainty that she held some grievance against him?

Next to Father's portrait lay the latest letter from my husband, a thinly veiled command to return at once to his house and bring my father's money with me. I recalled Mother's last words to me, her complaint that I had failed as a wife because I neglected my duties to my husband. How could she chide me, when she had found fault with a husband who never gave her a moment's anxiety, who was faithful, steadfast, industrious, loving, everything my husband was not? No. I acknowledged no duty to the man who has forced me to live these ten years in the madhouse of his cupidity, perversion, and lust. The fire in the grate burned low, but I took no notice. Another smoldered in my heart. I sat late in the cold room tending it, feeding it, until sparks ignited the dry tinder of my resentment, and it was as if I were sitting in a furnace.

~

There is no escape, yet how can I resign myself, when the world that is denied me tantalizes me at every turn. In the afternoon, as I stood with my sleeves rolled up, supervising the housecleaning, I received a note from my aunt inviting me to supper. *Joel Borden called this afternoon,* she wrote on the back of the card. *He will join us after supper to offer you his condolences.*

'Go to my aunt's at once,' I bade Peek. 'Tell her I will come at seven. And ask her for the loan of her black cashmere shawl.' Then I had Sarah leave off beating the carpets and spend the rest of the day washing and drying my hair.

Stupidly I enjoyed an inappropriate euphoria, as if I were going to attend some festive occasion, but as soon as I was seated next to my uncle in my aunt's dining room, I came to my senses. He had just returned from visiting a planter for whom he is factor and was still much burdened by the shock of Mother's sudden death. He took my hand in one of his, dabbing his handkerchief to his eyes with the other, and avowed the well-known scientific fact that Creoles are rarely taken by the yellow fever. This was the reason my mother had given for declining his invitation to their house

96

on the lake. My aunt, teary-eyed, pointed out that she had lost a cousin in the epidemic of 1822. How fortunate, my uncle observed, that I had arrived in time to bid my mother farewell.

Every mention of Mother causes me to relive the last minutes of her life, which leaves me speechless, gripped by panic, but it would not do for me to beg for a new subject. Joel would doubtless speak of nothing but the pain of my loss, of his sincere attachment to and affection for my mother. What would he think if I said I'd rather hear the gossip from the latest fête he had attended? I was quiet through supper, eating little, which my aunt and uncle did not remark upon, attributing low spirits and lack of appetite to my bereavement. At last we took our coffee into the drawing room, the bell rang, and a servant showed Joel into the room.

What a strange effect the sight of him had upon me. He looked strong, masculine, with that combination of languor and gaiety that is so appealing, yet his features were composed in an expression of sympathy that was unmistakably sincere. As his eyes met mine I found no trace of his habitual irony; only sadness and a tender care for my feelings. He came to me at once, holding out his hands. As I rose to meet him, I was weakened by an unexpected surge of grief, so that I clutched his hands for support. A thousand regrets crowded my brain, a hard sob broke from my throat, and tears streamed from my eyes. The impossibility of collapsing in Joel's embrace drove me back into my chair. There, bent over my knees and still clinging to his hands, I gave myself over to a storm of weeping. Joel released one hand to stroke my cheek, my hair, murmuring softly, 'My poor Manon, my poor, dear girl.' Through my sobs I heard my aunt say, 'She has been marvelously brave,' and then my uncle, after blowing his nose into his handkerchief, reminded Joel that it was unusual for a Creole to contract the yellow fever, and very odd of my mother to have succumbed to it. I regained control of myself and sat up, concentrating on extracting my handkerchief from my sleeve. 'Please forgive me,' I said.

'Always,' Joel said.

'There is nothing to forgive in natural feeling,' my aunt said. My uncle got up and went to the sideboard, taking out glasses. He poured a brandy with water for me, which he pronounced 'strengthening,' and two more without water for himself and Joel. 'Just a thimbleful of my berry cordial,' my aunt requested. Joel brought my glass to me and took a chair next to my aunt. Our conversation lingered upon the sadness of the occasion, then gradually moved to my plans for the future. 'What will you do with the house?' Joel inquired. 'It is such a sweet little place. I have spent many happy hours visiting there.'

'It would be a shame to part with it,' my uncle said.

'I'll close it up for now,' I said.

'It will make an excellent pied-à-terre,' my aunt suggested.

'It would indeed,' Joel said. 'With such a charming situation, perhaps your husband can be tempted to leave his sugarcane more often and join us here for the season.'

I took a good swallow of brandy, looking at Joel over the rim of the glass. Was it possible that he hadn't guessed how I felt about my husband? Or was his remark just politesse, intended to distract my aunt and uncle? His eyes met mine, thoughtful, interested, there was a trace of a smile on his lips.

'My husband dislikes New Orleans,' I said.

~

Joel's casual remark was much in my thoughts as I went through Mother's clothes, sorting some for charity and some for alteration. I had only a day to pack and close the house before my return to a place I hated for a duration I couldn't anticipate. I felt like a prisoner who has been led from his dark cell into the daylight, shown a gay, lively, sunny world, and told, all this is yours, and whenever you can persuade your jailer to accompany you, you may see it again. As I worked, nostalgia and remorse visited me by turns, making each decision a kind of torture, as if a kerchief's or an earring's fate had momentous implications for my own. Peek and Sarah were in and out, taking up carpets, putting covers on the furniture, polishing silver and storing it in felt bags. What will become of me? I thought, turning a garnet brooch over and over in my hand. I could remember the exact shape and size of the box it came in, the deep wine color of the velvet bow, and my father's amused glance in my direction as Mother pulled the ribbon apart eagerly. How had I moved so relentlessly from that bright moment to this one?

In the evening I dined with my aunt and we discussed my arrangements for the morrow. As I was leaving, she insisted on sending a servant with a lantern to accompany me back to the cottage, which was hardly necessary as the streets were well lit and the distance but a few blocks, heavily patrolled. It was a clear, chilly night, and as I passed beneath my neighbors' balconies I could hear the muted sounds of talking and laughing, the occasional shout of pleasure as someone won at cards or delighted the company with a bit of scandalous gossip. How plain and quiet my own little house seemed in comparison, yet I felt again a pleasurable twinge of ownership as I put the key in the lock and opened the door into the darkened parlor. I lit the lamp and closed the shutter behind me. The room had a ghostly, abandoned look to it already. The furniture was covered in loose cream-colored cases, the grate was swept and dry. Peek had gone to her new mistress, and Sarah, I presumed, was asleep. I passed into my bedroom, which is never entirely dark, as the light from the street filters through the shutters. My nightdress was laid out upon the chair, the pitcher filled with water, the bed linens turned back invitingly. I undressed quickly, and slipped beneath the quilt. Tomorrow, I thought, I will not find so welcome a resting place.

But I had scarcely closed my eyes when my drifting thoughts were focused upon the sound of whispering. At first it seemed to be coming from my pillow. One voice, then another, then a pause. I turned onto my back and lay still, listening. There was nothing. From far off I heard a horse's hooves approaching the corner, turning off toward the Place d'Armes. I closed my eyes. At once the whispering began again. The voice was urgent this time. Was it a man or a woman? No matter how I concentrated, I couldn't make out one word. It was coming from the floor. After a pause the other voice answered at some length. I sat up in the bed. Was it the floor or the wall? This one sounded like a woman. She was vexed, insistent. I slipped out of the bed and knelt on the bare floor. The voice stopped; there was no answer. A minute passed in which I heard only my own breathing. Just as I decided to get back into the bed, the second voice – I thought it must be a man – began again, lowered, placating, attempting to calm the first. It was coming from the wall, of course. There was a narrow alley between the cottage and the larger town house next door. Yet I was sure the sound was rising up through the boards between my knees. The space beneath the house was open on that side, but it was low, a man would have to crouch to get in there. Whisper, whisper. At length I made out the word 'afraid,' and another word repeated, which was either 'never' or 'better.' I dropped onto my hands and pressed my ear against the floor. At once the voice fell silent.

I'm going mad, I thought.

PART THREE

~

Insurrection

I hoped my husband would be occupied with his roofing project and I might at least have the leisure to change from my traveling clothes without seeing him, but as soon as we made the last turn into the drive there he was, stamping up and down on the porch, waving a walking stick which he clearly did not require. He was shouting at Mr Sutter, who sat astride his horse. In the next moment this gentleman tore off at a gallop, charging past us without a word as if pursued by the devil. My husband came to the steps to attend our arrival.

He was wearing a rumpled white suit without a cravat, riding boots, and an oversized planter's hat that squashed his red hair into a clump above his eyebrows. The sight of him was like a door slamming in my face. I even heard the catch of the latch, though perhaps it was only Sarah's baby swallowing hard. Sarah had made a paste of corn bread in her palm and was feeding the child from her fingertips. The creature couldn't seem to get enough of it. I noticed two white teeth coming in to its lower jaw. As I watched, it smacked its lips and gave me an absurdly cheerful grin. It would find little to be happy about in being weaned, I thought, and Sarah's long face told me she thought so too.

The driver reined in the horses and the rocking of the carriage smoothed out as they slowed to a walk. We were close enough for my husband to take off his hat and wave it at us. 'I just want to turn around and go back,' I said to no one. Sarah stuffed a last bit of paste into the baby's mouth and brushed the remains off over the side of the carriage. We came to a halt, the driver leaped from his seat, and in a moment we stood in the dirt facing one another. The welcome-home scene. Only let it be brief, I thought.

'Thank heaven you are safe,' my husband exclaimed, relieving me of my traveling case. 'I have been worried half to death.' Sarah pulled down the sack of Mother's linens and slipped past us into the house. The slave's blessing, I thought, forever exempt from the duties of greeting. 'I'm safe enough,' I said to my husband. 'But I'm very tired. If you don't mind, I'll go straight to my room and rest until supper.'

'Of course,' he said, shadowing me up the steps and through the door in a kind of anxious, ridiculous dance. 'But I must inform you of the report I have just received from Mr Sutter. A group of runaways has organized at Pass Manchac. Their plan is to march downriver picking up recruits along the way. They mean to join another group at Donaldsonville. They have called in the militia there. I'm surprised you weren't warned by patrols on the road. Mr Sutter said a slave at Overton informed the overseer of the plot yesterday. The revolt is planned for this very night.'

'And this informer is a free man today,' I snapped. 'Doesn't it ever occur to anyone that these plots only exist in the brains of malcontents who have realized they can get their freedom by scaring us out of our wits!'

This silenced him long enough for me to get to the stairs. I went up to my room without further comment and found Sarah unpacking, the baby already asleep in its crate. 'Leave that,' I said. 'Go and tell Delphine to make me a tisane; my head is splitting.' As she went out, I collapsed in the rocking chair. I fell to thinking of my husband's remark about the militia. Indeed we had seen no patrols, no other carriage to speak of. We saw one negro riding a mule and another leading a goat by a bit of rope. The epidemic was over in the city, the weather was fine, yet mile after mile the river road was empty and still. Had this rumor so engaged the population that they were afraid to move?

If there really was a conspiracy north of us, and they intended to meet up with cohorts in Donaldsonville, they would have to cross the river. And how would they do this? The narrowest stretch and the most reliable ferry was just south of our property. Did they plan to commandeer the ferry?

Sarah came in with the tray, which she set on the side table. I watched her back as she poured out the tea and stirred in the sugar. It struck me that she knew more about this story than I did, that she and Delphine could probably name the informer as well as the leader of the runaways. When she brought me the cup, I studied her face, her lowered eyes, her expressionless mouth. She was feeling sullen, I concluded.

107

'He'll be locking us up tonight, I gather,' I said, taking the cup, my eyes still on her face. She gave me a sudden penetrating look, then turned away. I drank my tea. A blade of anxiety sliced through the pain in my head, laying it open and raw. In Sarah's look I had read the same question I had in my own mind: How much do you know?

⁓

What did we eat that night? It seems a place to start. There was a gumbo, but what kind? It was the last pleasurable moment; Sarah lifting the lid of the tureen, and the delicious aroma filling the room. My aunt's cook, Ines, had served it often enough in the town, but in my opinion, no one made it better than Delphine. Was it chicken? After that there was another course and another, but what?

My husband droned on about the crop, as he thought it unwise to discuss the threat of a revolt before the servants, though there was only Sarah. He must have pictured Sarah telling Delphine or Rose, who would tell some passing hand, and thus it would make its way to the quarter, as if every negro in fifty miles didn't already know all about it.

I drank a good deal of wine. Sarah lit the lamps and served the coffee. The room seemed smoky to me, airless. When Sarah went out, my husband got up and bolted the shutters on the casements, which made it seem like a prison. 'I'd like a glass of port,' I said. My husband suggested that he had a good bottle in his office. I followed him there.

'Will you be joining the patrol?' I asked as he poured out a tablespoon of port.

'Not at first,' he said. 'They'll be starting near the Pass and pushing down this way.' He held the glass out to me.

'I'd like a little more than that, if you don't mind,' I said.

He looked puzzled, then took my meaning. 'I know these conspiracies must be torture to your nerves,' he said, filling the glass.

'On the contrary,' I said. 'It gives me something to think about besides my sewing.'

He ignored this remark. 'In truth, I'm reluctant to leave the house. I can't trust anyone to stand guard. If the informant told the truth, this plot has infiltrated every quarter from Pointe Coupée to the city on both sides of the river.' He opened his cabinet and took down two pistols.

'With the militia called out, they can have no chance of success,' I observed. 'What do they possibly hope to accomplish?'

'They just want to murder as many of us as they can,' he said. 'They don't think further than that.'

I sipped my port, thinking of them gathered around their fires of an evening, their rude passions inflamed by the wild talk of some preacher, planning how best to kill us all. And it wasn't just the field hands. In New Orleans, I had heard of an American lady who discovered her maid attempting to poison the entire household by lacing the sugar with arsenic. What benefit would her mistress's demise be to her, since she would only be sold again, perhaps to a more severe mistress? It puzzled me. 'I suppose it is just the numbers,' I said.

My husband cast me a questioning look, distracted by the business of tamping powder into one of his pistols.

'It is because they outnumber us so,' I explained. 'They don't understand why they can't do whatever they please.'

'It is because they are fiendish brutes,' my husband said.

I raised my eyebrows. 'Perhaps you are right,' I said.

He laid the pistol down and gave me his attention. 'There is another matter I wish to speak with you about, Manon. Will you hear me out?'

My inheritance, I thought. I was about to find out how he planned to squander my father's money. 'I'm at your convenience,' I said.

He raised one leg so that he was half-sitting on the end of his desk. 'While you were away, I thought a greal deal of you. More than I do when you are here.'

'"Absence makes . . ."' I waved my hand at the rest.

'It wasn't that. It was that I knew, if you could have your own way, you would never return.'

This straightforward statement of the simple truth took me by surprise. I set my glass on the side table and drew in a breath. The opportunity for honest exchange between us was rare and I determined to take advantage of it to advance a plan, a dream, really, that I had formulated on the long drive back from town. 'No,' I said. 'If it were not my obligation I would never return here.'

He narrowed his eyes as if my confession pained him, though it couldn't have been unexpected, as he'd just remarked upon his certainty of my preference. 'Isn't there some way we can close this rift between us and live as husband and wife?' he pleaded.

Clearly he imagined there was something he could say that would persuade me to invite him into my bedroom, an idea that had no appeal to me at all. 'No,' I said.

He studied me a moment, evidently mystified by my coldness. 'It's that simple, is it?' he said.

'It is, yes,' I said. 'But as you've brought up this "rift," as you call it, I do have a proposition regarding it.'

'I am willing to hear it,' he said.

'What I propose is that we agree to spend more time apart. Now that I have my mother's house, I could stay in town for the season. I will have to have a cook, as Peek is gone, and I would take Sarah with me, so you might do as Mother so often advised you and buy a proper butler.'

'I thought the loss of your mother might soften your heart toward me,' he said. 'I see it has had the opposite effect.'

'I am orphaned,' I said. 'Who will defend my interests if I don't defend them myself?'

'I will never agree to your proposal,' he said.

I expected this response, had indeed planned for it, holding my high card to my chest like a proper gambler. 'And if I were to leave Sarah here,' I said. 'What then?'

He brought his hand to his chin and began pulling at his mustache, his eyes fixed on me with resolute puzzlement. He could see it. He would have Sarah to himself and I would be gone. He mulled it over with the same expression he gave the menu on those rare occasions when we had dined at restaurants together; the prospect of making the wrong choice vexed him sorely. 'You are my wife,' he declared at last.

'That is my misfortune,' I said.

He stood up, returning his attention to his pistols. 'I don't see that we can afford to keep your mother's house,' he said. 'I plan to have my lawyer seek out a buyer for it.'

My resolution failed me and my eyes filled with useless tears. 'No,' I said. 'I won't consent to that.'

He smiled indulgently, turning his pistol over in his hands. 'Well,' he said. 'Don't cry, Manon. We will discuss the matter. There's plenty of time.'

'It's *my* house,' I protested.

He didn't bother to answer this assertion, thereby making me more conscious of how hollow it was. I dried my eyes against my sleeve.

'I suppose we should first see if we can get through this night without incident,' he said. 'I want you and Sarah to stay in your room, but leave the door open. I plan to pass the night on the couch on the landing. I want to be able to hear you should you call for help.'

This struck me as an idiotic plan, but I felt too defeated to object. I finished off the port and stood up, not surprised that I was dizzy. My husband came to my side and tried to take my arm, but I pulled away brusquely. He followed me a few steps, then fell back. 'I have work to finish here,' he said, as if I were interested in his plans. 'I will come up when I have made sure the kitchen is locked.'

I dragged myself up the stairs. In my room I found Sarah spreading Mother's shawl out on her mattress. The baby lay on its stomach near her feet, trying to crawl but getting nowhere. At least that one will be gone soon, I thought. I went to the window and looked out into the darkness. It was cool, clear. There was a damp breeze from the north that made me pull my own shawl tight over my chest. I

112

should close the window before I go to bed, I thought, or put on another blanket. I considered this trivial question for a few moments as I leaned on my elbows looking out at the stars. There was a gibbous moon. How fine it would be to walk out under the trees, but that, of course, was unthinkable. 'I don't see any signs of an uprising out here,' I said to amuse myself.

I glanced back at Sarah, who was on her knees, looking up at me, her eyebrows knit as if I'd addressed her in a language she didn't understand. I turned back to the night, chiding myself for having spoken facetiously. The truth was that at that moment I wanted nothing more than to pour out the tale of my unhappiness to someone who loved me, but there was no such person. He's going to sell my house, I thought, and I'll be trapped here until I die. I scanned the roots of the tree, recalling the night I'd seen a man there looking back at me. I'd told no one, partly from a wish that my silence might result in difficulty for my husband, partly from fear that he would seize on the information to increase his hysterical vigilance. My little circuit, I thought, from hope to fear and back again.

I heard a night bird cry and an answering call from near the kitchen. A dim light suffused the air in that direction; Delphine was awake, locked in there with Walter and Rose. He would turn the dogs loose outside before he came up. The quarter was under a strict curfew: no man, woman, or child would dare show his face until morning. All night the master would stride about his citadel, pointing his pistols at insects, breezes, and mice, and in the morning we would have breakfast as usual.

Another blanket, I decided. It was chilly and there were no mosquitoes. I would sleep without the bar. I turned to tell Sarah to take a blanket from the armoire. She was wrapping the baby tightly in her shawl. This struck me as curious. She passed a fold over its head so that it looked like an Indian baby such as I have seen in the market in town, attached to its mother's back by a leather strap. A papoose. That was what they called them. My eye fell upon the welcome sight of the blue bottle containing my sleeping tincture and I took a few steps to the table. I detected a motion at the doorway and turned to see what it was.

High against the jamb, the upper part of a black face with only one eye showing peered in at me. In the same moment I saw it, it slipped away, leaving me unsure of my own eyes. My thoughts scattered in every direction, seeking some reasonable explanation: my husband had decided to take a trustworthy guard into the house after all, or this was a messenger with important news from town. My body had no such fatuous doubts. The blood that rushed to my brain left my knees weak and my head as clear as a street swept by a hurricane. The event we all feared most had begun and there was to be no escape from it. I slumped against the bed, opened my mouth, but no sound came out. Sarah got up, cradling the bundle she had made of her baby. She went to the window. When I looked back at the doorway, there was the single eye again, watching me.

'Sarah?' I said softly, turning slowly, cautiously, to the window. She was leaning out, holding the baby close to her chest, looking first one way, then the other. Soundlessly she held the bundle out over the sill and dropped it. I

114

listened for the thump, the cry, but there was nothing.

What did it mean? She turned from the window, her eyes wide, looking past me at the apparition in the doorway. She saw it too. My mind was not made easier by this revelation. I turned back, still clinging to the bedpost, though I felt my strength returning. The face was there, a little more of it now, a bit of the nose and cheek. How long did he intend to spy upon us in this absurd fashion. 'What are you doing here?' I asked. How calm my voice was!

For answer he stepped boldly into the doorway. He was a tall man, very black, dressed in a loose cotton shirt and rough breeches, no shoes. In one hand he held a cane cutter, in the other a butchering knife. He stood with his feet turned out, his shoulders slumped, and his eyes strangely unfocused, as if presenting himself for inspection. I didn't think I had seen him before. He was a field hand, a runaway from somewhere, there would be no reasoning with him. And, indeed, no compelling argument sprang to my mind. Where was my husband with his pistols? His obsession had finally materialized, and he was nowhere to be found. It crossed my mind that he was already dead.

'He not alone,' Sarah said, and I replied, 'No, I think not. Come and stand close to me.'

She moved to my side and there we stood, while the air grew thick with the inevitability of murder. We heard the first shot, a shout, then another shot. Our captor appeared unconcerned. Everything was still; only the curtain rustled in the breeze. All at once the scratching in the wall started up, loud and urgent, as if the silence was too much for the rodent to bear. I could hear Sarah's shallow breathing next to me, and in my ear my own racing pulse. The man leaned back into the hall, looking toward the landing. A voice called up the stairs, 'Bring them down.' He stepped back, motioning us into the hall with his cane knife.

My impulse was to run, but where? My husband had taken great care to lock the house, evidently sealing us in with our murderers. Sarah took up the lamp and preceded me out to the landing. Our captor followed closely, his shadow leaping up the wall in front of me so that I felt surrounded by him. At the landing he said, 'Wait.' I stopped. Sarah turned back, and we both watched as he examined the spyglass. A cough drew my attention down to where the light from the dining room pooled at the foot of the stairs. Another man was there, smaller, blacker, holding a pistol at his side and smiling up at me. 'Come down now, ladies,' he said. 'And come slow.'

I rested my hand on the rail and went down, pausing at each step. Sarah came behind me, holding up the lamp so that I was outlined in light. My head was bursting with questions. Where was my husband? What had happened to Sarah's baby? Was Delphine safe in the kitchen? How many men were there? How did they get in, and, above all, how could I escape? At the end of the hall I saw that the front door was open and a third man stood in the frame. He held a rifle against his shoulder and looked out at the darkness. The one who had spoken, whom I took to be their captain, stepped back to let me pass. 'Just go right on in there,' he said, indicating the dining room. I did as he instructed and received a hard shock: there were four more of them. One was sprawled in a side chair, shirtless, while another knelt before him, wrapping a length of cloth around the seated man's bleeding arm. They had opened all the shutters and casements. Another man, gripping a short knife, leaned in one doorway looking out while the last, armed with a sword, stood just outside the room looking in. Sarah passed me and set the lamp on the sideboard. More lamps were on the table, along with the remains of a ham and half a loaf of bread, thrown there without the bother of plates. They'd cut into the ham with their knives, leaving deep gashes in the wood. They've destroyed that table, I thought, which made me angry. My anger made me bold. I addressed their captain, who stood blocking the door. 'Where is my husband?'

The captain came into the room, pulled out a chair, and sat down, giving me a rueful smile. 'Thas just what I like to know,' he said. 'He clipped my bird here' – he lifted his hand to the wounded man – 'and run right out the front door.'

So he had escaped. 'Then he will alert the patrol,' I said.

The wounded man laughed. 'I don't think so,' the captain said.

'He got a load of shot in his backside,' the wounded man said.

'I'm thinking your husband laying close by, missy,' the captain said. 'He wily and he won't leave his woman. I'm thinking he come right to us.'

'You should run while you still can,' I said.

For answer the captain examined his pistol, turning it over in his hands. It was my husband's, and he used it just as my husband did, as an aid to thought. I looked at Sarah, who stood with her back to the sideboard as if she expected to be called upon to serve coffee. There was a shout outside. The man with the sword rushed across the porch and plunged into the azaleas.

'That be him now,' the captain said.

There were more shouts, the sound of scuffling; a man backed into the porch, crouched down, then lurched forward, falling headlong across the bricks. 'I got 'im,' a voice cried, and another man laughed. 'What is it?' the same voice said. The captain got up and went to the doors as the guard came in holding out before him the naked, filthy, squirming, screaming body of Walter. 'Be careful now,' the guard said. 'He bite.'

'Turn him loose,' the captain ordered. As soon as his feet hit the ground, the boy tried to dive back outside, but he was redirected by a kick from the guard and took off around the dining table.

'Is this one yours, missy?' the captain asked me.

'He a little yellow monkey,' the wounded man said.

Walter had spotted the ham and was trying to pull himself onto the table. The captain approached him, broke off a piece of bread from the loaf, and offered it to the creature, who shook his head vehemently, emitting a high-pitched whine and stretching out his arms to the ham.

'He don't want no bread,' the wounded man observed.

'What his name?' the captain said to me.

'Walter,' I said.

'Tell him to stop that noise,' he said. I shrugged.

'He don't hear,' Sarah said.

The captain regarded her closely, drew the obvious

118

conclusion, and laughed. 'Miss High Yellow got herself a little redheaded monkey,' he said. He raised the butt of the pistol and brought it down with a sharp crack across the side of Walter's head. The child crumpled to the carpet, kicked his legs up, moaned once, then lay still.

No one spoke. I realized that my palms were damp, my mouth strangely dry. I glanced at Sarah, who had laid her hand across her mouth and closed her eyes, and then at the wounded man. His attendant had finished the bandaging. The captain went to him and petted his head. 'How bad is it?' he said. The man looked up into his face with a bemused smile, raised his arm a few inches, and winced. 'Not too bad,' he said.

'Where is this devil done clipped my Crow?' the captain asked, strutting away to join the two at the doors. Walter moved his arm, opened his eyes, but made no sound. So he wasn't dead.

The captain stood between his men, gazing out into the night. He was a trim, bandy-legged man with a big head, two shades darker and half a foot shorter than his companions. He was running straight to the gallows and he knew it. All I could hope was that I might live to see that day.

We could hear the unmistakable sound of a horse's hooves coming across the grass, fast, at a gallop. 'Damn,' the captain said and ran onto the porch, waving his pistol. One of the men followed; the other turned on us, jabbing his knife menacingly. 'Get yourselves together there,' he said, pointing to the table. Sarah and I did as he directed and stood with our backs to the table, not daring to look at each other. We heard a shot alongside the house. The

119

man who had been guarding the front door ran past the casements.

The horse was getting very close; in the next moment I expected to see it come crashing into the room. I felt a pull at my skirt and looked down at Walter. His mouth was opening and closing and a stream of drool poured onto the carpet.

A torch went up outside, and I saw the horse hurtling toward the house, its big head lifted, fighting the bit. Just as it was about to collide with the porch columns, it veered, pitching into the azaleas. It was my husband's bay gelding, riderless, the reins tangled in the saddle. Quickly it recovered its footing, backed out of the bushes, and stood trembling on the drive. The torch came behind it.

Every one of us in that room stood transfixed, trying to make out the exact positions of the two men walking in the torchlight. One was the captain, his chest thrust out, his hands resting on his hips. The other, walking with an odd, shambling gait, holding the torch high in one hand, and in the other a pistol pointed steadily at the head of his captive, was my husband.

~

They passed the horse, which ambled away into the darkness, and came across the drive to the house. As they entered the room, my husband thrust the torch at the remaining guard, who backed away nervously. The men were all riveted by the pistol, but I was fascinated by the change in my husband. He was smeared from head to toe with mud

120

and blood. His neck was gashed and blood had poured down his chest, soaking his shirt, which was torn nearly to shreds. His hair was wild, standing out on one side, packed flat with mud on the other. His eyes burned with excitement. He jabbed the pistol at his captive's temple and said, 'Now just don't move.' The wounded man sat forward in his chair and said, 'Oh, Lord.'

'Just do what he say,' the captain ordered.

'That's right,' my husband said. 'Manon, come stand behind me.' I did as he said. He's going to save me, I thought, and a great perplexity came upon me. I was looking at his back, which was bloody from the waist down. Everyone was still but Walter, who groaned once, clutched his head in his hands, and sat up.

'Now we will walk out the door,' my husband said. 'Just the three of us.' I looked back at Sarah, who was edging away from the table, her eyes on the wounded negro. Did my husband mean Sarah? But no, he meant the captain; that was the three of us. My husband pressed the barrel of the pistol into the captain's ear and backed him toward the door.

Then we were outside, walking on the drive. The horse stood farther off on the lawn, calmly ripping up grass. As my eyes grew accustomed to the dark, I went ahead, pulling my skirt up about my legs. There was one thought in my head, and that was to get to the horse. The captain was speaking. I dimly apprehended the purport of his message, that we were outnumbered, that it made little difference whether he was killed or not, my husband would not survive, he was a dead man.

121

'I am. You are,' my husband replied. 'It's just a question of who goes first.'

'Thas right,' the captain said. 'Thas right.'

Perfect, I thought. They are in agreement.

The torch was growing dimmer with every second. I could make out the dining room doors and someone inside moving toward them. Where was the one with the rifle, who had run into the night at the sound of the horse? I scanned the bushes. The farther we got from the house, the darker it became. If I did get to the horse, which way should I ride? I heard voices from the house, raised, anxious, then a crash as if someone had dropped a tray of glasses. The sound of rapid footsteps came toward us across the lawn. My husband stopped, looked back, still keeping his pistol close to the captain's ear, and I looked too. An eerie pale figure whirled toward us, its feet barely touching the ground.

After that everything happened quickly, though it felt as if time itself had fallen open like a book, and each new impression was completed, even recollected, before the next began. Walter, for of course it was he, threw himself at my husband's legs with such force that he stumbled, cursing; the captain took advantage of his imbalance to knock the pistol from his hand. I fell to my knees, trying to reach the pistol. The captain kicked me in the face so hard that I sprawled upon the ground. Suddenly there were others running in all directions. A guard appeared, his butcher knife slicing the air before him, and gave chase to my husband, who had shaken Walter from his legs and was running. I got to my hands and knees. Sarah appeared outside the dining room doors, her hair and skirts flying, headed for the side of the house. My husband disappeared into a copse of crepe myrtle, his pursuer followed. I got to my feet and took a few steps toward the horse. The captain, having recovered the pistol, aimed it at me, shouting, 'Stay there.' Another figure came running out from alongside the house, Sarah shouted, and the two ran to one another. Sarah changed directions, barely breaking her stride, and continued in the direction of the horse. 'Where is the *man*?' the captain complained to me. Another guard, an enormous man brandishing a cane cutter, came lumbering up from nowhere, closing in on Sarah. To elude him she turned toward me. My face and chin were wet. I put my hand to my cheek and felt a gash in the flesh. It must have been his toenail, I thought. Blood was flooding my mouth; in the fall I'd bitten through my lip. As Sarah approached, her pursuer paused to light a torch.

In the blaze of light much was revealed. Walter collided with Sarah and clung to her skirt. I saw her face, her rage and desperation as she struggled to free herself. 'Let me go,' she cried, kicking the creature, who released her, wailing in distress. Something was moving in the darkness just beyond the light. Sarah turned, pointed into the blackness, and shouted to the guard, who was very near her, 'He there.' The captain walked away from me, blocking my view for a moment. In the next I saw a hellish tableau.

My husband was on his knees, struggling to rise. The big man held him by his hair. Sarah stood near him, clutching her baby close against her shoulder, her eyes on the cane knife, which the man raised high over his head.

In the next moment the knife came down. There was the sickening sound of steel breaking through bone, and my husband's head dropped forward into his chest at an impossible angle. The captain hailed his comrade, who stepped back to admire his handiwork. For a moment my husband was still, as if he might stand up; then he collapsed sidelong onto the grass. Sarah was running straight toward me. In my shock I failed to see that I stood between her and the horse, but by the time she was close I understood and reached out to stop her, catching her by the elbow. She turned on me in a fury, tearing at my face with her free hand, her sharp nails digging into my already wounded cheek. 'They won't hurt you,' I said. 'Let me go first. They'll kill me if you don't.' She kicked me, knocking me aside, but I caught her again by the shoulder. She spun around quickly, loosening my grip, and sank her teeth into my hand. I cried out, released her, and she left me behind, running full out for the horse. I went after her, nearly catching up at one point. As I ran, I could hear the men laughing. Sarah outdistanced me, sprang into the saddle, startling the horse so that he reared, came down, sidestepped one way, then the other. Somehow, clutching the baby across her stomach, she gathered up the reins, gave a hard kick and took off, her skirt billowing out behind her.

The sound of the horse's hooves tearing up the grass, the sight of her bent low over the animal's neck, confounded me. Absurd questions distracted me from my own peril: Where had she learned to ride like that? What direction would she take? Was she going for help? Then the sound of human feet pounding the ground restored me to what was left of my senses. I knew only enough to run, to keep running. I heard the captain shout, the report of the pistol, which seemed not loud, far away, yet at the same time there was a searing, astounding pain in my shoulder, and I understod that I had been hit.

I kept running. There was no cover. I had no idea where I was, what direction to take. The house was somewhere behind me, overrun with murderers. If I could get to the quarter, surely someone would protect me. It was black, the ground riddled with roots that tripped me and nettle grass that cut my feet like razors. Somewhere along the way I'd lost my flimsy shoes. Gradually the ground seemed to decline beneath my feet, the grass thinned, and the earth became wet and cool. At last there were branches, bushes, places to hide. I could hear them still behind me, still in pursuit, so I pressed on, feeling my way by clutching at limbs and seeking the driest ground with my feet. My skirt caught on every bramble. I paused long enough to pull it up between my legs and knot it above my knees. Insects swarmed around my head; my hand closed on something sinuous and leathery. I recoiled, losing my balance, and sat down hard on a tree root. I could hear the men's voices, not as close, but not far enough. Keep going, I told myself, and got to my feet. Something skittered across the ground; a bat whirred overhead. I took a few steps, holding my hands out before me. I was standing in a few inches of water. Wrong way, I thought, and changed direction, but the next steps only brought the icy water to my knees. Wrong way, I told myself again, turning once more. This time my feet found less water, more mud; mud to my shins.

I slogged through it. My shoulder had turned into a throbbing mass; the pain made me groan with every step. Insects flew into my mouth and eyes, buzzing louder and louder until I couldn't hear anything else. They will eat me alive, I thought.

I would die where I stood. Then miraculously a solution occurred to me, one I'd seen the negroes use, to my disgust. I bent down and plunged my hands into the cool mud, then smeared it over my face, my arms, and into my hair. Put it on thick, I told myself, squatting to get another handful. The buzzing subsided. I went on, feeling my way. I was out of the mud on soft ground, then my feet found a patch of cool ferns that felt like a carpet laid beneath my feet. I stopped, listened, heard a variety of noises, but none of them voices. They wouldn't waste what little time they had left in this world to search the swamp for a wounded woman, I thought. A powerful lethargy swept over me. My legs were leaden; I could not lift my head. A little farther, I told myself. I could make out the trunk of a big oak just ahead, as wide around as a cabin. I staggered to it, stumbling in the maze of its roots, which sprawled out in every direction, making various moss-covered nests. I sat down in one of these, close to the trunk. It seemed a perfect resting spot. When I moved my arm, the pain made me cry out. My dress was stuck to my back from my shoulder to my waist. How much blood have I lost? I wondered. I heard a rushing sound overhead, a crack of branches in the brush nearby. I could not remember why I was in the forest at night. My head ached. I opened and closed my mouth. It felt as if my jaw was broken. I could see Sarah's face, her lips pulled

126

back over her teeth like a snarling dog as she struggled with me. 'They will kill me,' I said, but she wasn't listening, or didn't hear. No, I thought. She heard me well enough. It was her hope that they would kill me.

'But I'm still alive,' I said with satisfaction. Then it seemed the darkness around me was as much behind my eyes as in front of them, and I gave up trying to see through it.

~

When I opened my eyes again, I was looking at a black hand. The light was soft, pinkish, and there was a wheezing sound coming from somewhere behind me; it sounded like a torn bellows. I moved my fingers and understood that the hand was my own. The mud on my palm cracked open, revealing the pale flesh beneath. My mouth was as dry as the mud, my head a circlet of pain that emanated down, then out to my shoulder, where it became a fire. When I tried to sit up, nothing happened. I blinked, gazing up into the maze of limbs and leaves over my face. It must be just dawn, I thought. I tried turning onto my side, away from the burning shoulder. This time I was successful. I pulled myself up onto my good arm. I knew where I was, I remembered how I had gotten there. But what was this whistling at my back? Carefully I turned my head. I was reminded that my cheek was torn, my jaw in some new configuration that made it throb like an outraged heart. I looked down at a bruised and naked body curled in a hollow between two roots, its arms and legs drawn in close, the side of its head swollen, bloody, and bruised, its mouth open, snoring as peacefully as if the moss was a feather bed. It was Walter.

A racket of blue jays in a bush nearby made me want to clutch my head, but my right arm was unresponsive to my command. I noticed a thin stream running nearby. The water sparkled as the sun flushed over the tops of the bushes and bright rays pierced the forest from every direction. I grasped a low branch passing near my nest, and pulled myself to my feet. I was unsteady, I was in the purest agony, but I was on my feet.

'Wake up, Walter,' I said in a voice to rival the jays. Then I recalled that my sleeping companion wouldn't hear a gun fired next to his ear. How had he found me? Did he know his way in this place? I peeled a clump of mud from my hand and threw it at him, striking him on the leg. His eyes flew open, he coughed, then began to cry. I should have left well enough alone, I thought.

The stream probably ran toward the river. My way must be in the opposite direction. I took a step, then another; each one felt as if it might be the last. Walter sat up among the roots and babbled nonsense. 'Quiet,' I said, straining to see through to some wider area of light. A chameleon rushed past my feet, another stopped on the root in front of me and eyed me, once from each side of its head. A world of idiots and monsters, I thought, and I left to tell the tale.

The air was damp, and the cold penetrated to my bones. It seemed to me there was a clearing beyond a bramble bush, but I couldn't see how to get to it, as the bush was as long as a city block. Walter got to his feet and walked off in the other direction, toward what I took to be the river. Should I follow? He disappeared beyond the next tree, then I heard rapid footsteps. Slowly, painfully, I made my way in his tracks, skirting a tangle of broken branches and vines, then around the thick trunk of a bay tree. I was standing on the lawn looking up at the side of the house. Walter ran ahead of me across the grass, toward what looked like a pile of clothing. The sun broke over the roof of the house, bathing the scene with a freshness utterly inappropriate to what it exposed. The air was bright, chilly, and still. I saw the cloud of flies rising above the crumpled body of my husband. Walter had reached it. He bent over the body and began struggling to lift the head, shrieking all the while.

Don't do that, I thought. Don't touch him. The front doors of the house stood open, the dining room casements were all ajar, but there was no sign of living occupants. So the field hands had got up with the bell and gone out to their work, blissfully unaware that their master lay with his head nearly off on the lawn. Mr Sutter had not come to join the fray; the vaunted patrol had skipped our house in its pursuit of the rebels. Was it possible?

I dragged myself toward the drive, pausing every few steps to get my breath. I thought I might die of thirst before I got to the door. If only Delphine is here, I thought. I went in through the hall, glancing in at the dining room just long enough to see that it was wrecked, chairs upended, broken glass everywhere, the remains of the ham mysteriously left on the carpet near the hall door. I went through the hall, out at the back, across the narrow yard to the kitchen door. It was closed. I tried the latch; it was locked. I leaned against it. 'Delphine,' I said. 'Are you there? Let me in.' The curtain at the narrow window moved, Rose peeked out, gave a shout, and dropped the curtain. 'Let me in,' I said again. 'I'm not a ghost. But I may be soon if you don't open this door.' The curtain moved again. This time Delphine looked out. 'Is that you, missus?' she said.

'I'm alive,' I said. 'They didn't kill me.' She pulled the bolt and the door swung out before me. 'Lord, missus,' Delphine said, leading me inside. 'What happen to you.'

'I got away,' I said. 'I hid in the woods. But they shot me.' I gestured to my shoulder. In the process I saw my mud-daubed arm, my torn and bloody sleeve, and I remembered that I was covered in mud. 'Get me some water,' I said, sinking into a chair at the table. 'I'm dying of thirst.'

The fire was up, there were pots already boiling, good smells of bread and meat. Delphine put a glass of water in front of me and I drank it at one gulp. 'More,' I said, holding out the glass. Rose brought the pitcher and filled it again. Delphine went to the kettle and poured hot water into a bowl, then brought it to the table and added some cool from the pitcher. She took a cloth, dropped it in the water, and wrung it out. 'I hardly knows where to start,' she said. I took the cloth and wiped my face, wincing when I found the gash in my cheek. 'Thas a bad cut,' Rose observed. Delphine was unfastening the back of my dress. 'All these bits of cloth stuck in the wound,' she said. 'It gonna hurt to clean this out.'

'I can't lift my arm,' I said.

We heard a whining sound coming from the house, and in a moment Walter stumbled into the yard. He was holding his face in his hands, weeping. His hands and bare chest were stained with dark blood. He stopped, took us in, and held out his arms, tears mixed with blood streaming down his face. His forehead was so swollen his eye was closed up.

'Poor chile,' Rose said, going to him. 'What they done to you?' She picked him up and he buried his face in her neck.

'He's crying because his father is out there dead on the lawn,' I said.

There was a brief hush in which everyone noticed that I had spoken of my husband as Walter's father. Delphine took the cloth from me and rinsed it in the basin. 'Master killed,' she said softly.

'Rose,' I said. 'Go down and find Mr Sutter. Tell him to come to the house at once.' Rose put the child down, handed him a piece of bread, and went out, glancing about the yard nervously, starting at the chickens. Walter sat near my feet, chewing his bread from one hand and picking at the dried mud between my toes with the other. 'Stop that,' I said, pulling my feet in under the chair.

∼

Mr Sutter was dead too. They had stopped at his house first, sneaked in a window, and cut his throat. When Rose got there she found the door wide open and Cato, the driver, standing on the porch. 'Don't go in,' he told her.

'Just tell missus Mr Sutter been murdered in his bed.'

'Send a boy for the doctor,' I told her on hearing this news, and she headed back to the quarter. Delphine was filling a tub with warm water. 'Best I cut that dress off you with the scissors,' she said.

'Just get it off,' I said wearily. 'I don't care how you do it.' She had unknotted the skirt and was cutting it up the front when we heard heavy footsteps coming rapidly through the house. 'Lock the door,' I said, but before Delphine could get off her knees, a deep male voice called out, 'Hallo. Is anyone here?'

Blessed Providence, I thought. There are still white men alive. 'In here,' I called out. 'In the kitchen.'

One by one they filed into the yard. There were four of them, dressed in vaguely military coats, high boots, armed with swords and pistols. Where were they when I needed them? Their eyes grew wide as they discovered me, sitting in my kitchen, covered in mud, my face swollen and bleeding, my useless arm cradled in my lap. I recognized one, an acquaintance of my husband, a lawyer named O'Malley. 'Mrs Gaudet,' he said solemnly. 'It is my unhappy duty to inform you that your husband has been murdered.'

I hardly knew whether to laugh or cry. It was as if I had been in a foreign country, a land where madness was the rule, and returned to find nothing changed but my own understanding. I glanced at Delphine. She looked dismayed, though her features were composed in an approximation of servility. She's worried about what will happen to her now, I thought. We all are. Every minute of every hour. Mr O'Malley stood waiting for my response. He was worried

I might have gone mad and he would have to deal with it. 'I know it,' I said calmly, to his obvious relief. 'I was there.'

~

It was hours before I spun together the threads of the various stories and produced a credible fabric. I hardly cared, but it was a kind of sewing, and I used it, as usual, to keep my mind off my own suffering, which was intense. First there was the pain occasioned by Delphine picking the bits of cloth from the wound in my shoulder and cleaning it with alcohol. When Dr Landry finally arrived, he admired her nursing skills and my endurance, then set about determining the outermost limits of the latter. The shots of brandy I downed at the start had worn off by the time he'd dug out three lead balls and announced there were only two to go. 'I can't stand one more second,' I cried. 'Don't you have something stronger than brandy?' He poured another glass. 'I've seen soldiers who could not hold up as well as you,' he said, a compliment for which I felt the greatest indifference. After what seemed an hour, he held up another ball in his tweezers and dropped it into the washbasin with a sigh. 'I'm going to have to leave the last one in, I'm afraid,' he said. 'It's buried too deep in the muscle.' I raised my good hand to wipe the perspiration from my forehead. 'That's the best news I've had in days,' I said. Then he gave me the worst, which was that I would never recover the use of my arm. One of the balls had chipped a bone and severed a tendon at the top of my shoulder. 'You'll be able to use your hand all right,' he said.

133

'Eventually you may be able to raise the arm a little.' While I reeled from this diagnosis, he took out his needle and thread and went to work on my face.

O'Malley and his men busied themselves putting the house to rights. They picked up my husband's body and moved it to the icehouse. Mr Sutter was brought there too, wrapped in a blanket so none of the hands could see him, as it is well known that the sight of a dead overseer agitates the negroes. Two of the patrol stayed downstairs all night, prowling about ceaselessly, though there was no danger of the insurrectionists returning. After wrecking the house and taking off everything from flatware to footstools, as if they intended to set up a plantation of their own down the way, they had marched to the river road in time to run right into the patrol.

The chase was violent and protracted, much of it in the bottomland, where mud and the darkness complicated the outcome. One of the patrol was shot in the leg, another stabbed through the eye. Four of the negroes, including the captain, were shot dead, the other two were captured and trussed for hanging. The patrol had passed half the night in pursuit and spent the other half moving the captives downriver, where they were joined by a second patrol coming north who informed them that a battle was raging in Donaldsonville and all men called. It was not until morning that Mr O'Malley recollected seeing my spoons gleaming in the mud and thought to investigate the Gaudet plantation.

When it was all over, they had captured fifty negroes; every one was shot or hanged in the next few days. Casualties among the planters were not heavy. There were a dozen injured and two murdered: my husband and his overseer, Mr Sutter.

~

The next morning my aunt came up from town; she was followed by a mule-drawn cart containing two coffins sent from Chatterly by my brother-in-law, Charles Gaudet. This gentleman arrived with his son Edmund in the afternoon. I refused to see anyone, as I was too sick to leave my bed, so all the arrangements fell to my aunt, which suited everyone. She sent me her own maid, a capable nurse, who administered different medicines and fed me soup, tea, and custard. Though it hurt to eat, I was ravenous. All day I listened to the front door opening and closing, the drone of voices, at first subdued, but, as the rooms filled and my aunt served a buffet dinner with quantities of wine, gradually more lively, occasionally punctuated by laughter. My aunt looked in on me every hour to describe the progress of the funeral. All the planters for miles along the river attended, for even those who had disliked my husband, or scarcely made his acquaintance, understood the importance of standing at his graveside. In the afternoon they walked out to the cemetery for a brief ceremony, then came back to the house for more food and wine. I heard it all through a curtain of pain. Toward dark they began to drift away, and so did I, into a feverish sleep. When I woke it was morning and my aunt was sitting next to my bed with an envelope in her lap.

'How are you feeling, my dear?' she said.

There was an agreeable moment of clarity in which I knew that my husband was dead and buried, followed by a blast of pain so powerful it chased out every fact save itself. 'Never worse,' I said.

'What can I give you?' She gestured to the table of medicines.

'Just a little water.'

She poured a glass and brought it to my lips. 'Is the letter for me?' I said when I had swallowed a few sips.

'It is from Joel Borden. He particularly asked me to bring it to you.'

'Let me see it,' I said. My aunt proffered the envelope and I made an awkward business of opening it in my lap. I shook out the page and read:

My dearest Manon,
The enormity of your misfortune is so staggering I hardly know what words to write. First your dear mother, and now this horrible misfortune and loss. If I can be of any help to you in days to come, please call upon me. If not, I hope it will be some small comfort to you to receive the sympathy and affection of your devoted friend,

Joel

'This is so kind,' I said. Then the stabbing pain in my face reminded me of my injuries. I laid my palm against the bandage over my cheek. 'What will I look like when my face is healed?'

'Dr Landry is an excellent surgeon,' my aunt assured me. 'He put twenty-seven stitches in my Ines's forehead and there is barely a scar.'

'But my mouth,' I said, probing the spiky threads that ran from inside my lip to the base of my chin.

My aunt made no reply. Perhaps she thought me frivolous, though I doubt any woman can entertain the possibility of disfigurement with equanimity. I folded the letter and slipped it back into the envelope. I had to use my left hand to move my right hand into a useful position. What would look worse, I wondered, my face or my arm hanging limp at my side?

'Manon,' my aunt said, 'where is Sarah?'

'She hasn't come back?'

'No one has seen her.'

'Delphine must know.'

'No.'

I looked at my hand. There were three bruised marks just behind my thumb. 'She bit me,' I said.

'Merciful heaven,' my aunt said.

'She took my husband's horse and rode off. I begged her to let me get away, but she wouldn't.'

'Then she has run away,' my aunt concluded.

'But where?' I exclaimed.

'She can't have gotten far. She is probably hiding in town. It would surprise me if Mr Roget didn't know something of her whereabouts. I shall write to your uncle to make inquiries at once.'

My husband is dead, I thought. Why would she run now, when she was safe from him? It didn't make sense.

'She has her baby with her,' I said.

'That will make it all the easier to find her.'

I could see her face again, her lips drawn back over her teeth, her eyes crazed and glowing in the torchlight as she pointed out my husband to his murderers and stood by until the blade had descended upon his neck.

'Yes,' I agreed. 'We'll find her.'

~

I sent for Delphine to quiz her about Sarah, and to find out what she knew about that night. She said she had gone into the yard after supper to throw out the dishwater and when she came back she saw three of the runaways standing in the kitchen. So they were already in the house when I was speaking to my husband in his office. Delphine slipped out of the yard and crept along the back of the house to my window, where she threw pebbles until Sarah looked out. 'I tole her what I seen,' Delphine said, 'and she say for me to wait 'til she pass me her Nell, so I hid by the wall. Then she wrap up the chile and pass her down to me.'

'But I looked out then,' I said. 'I didn't see anyone.'

'I seen you, missus,' Delphine said. 'But I was 'fraid to speak out and I figure Sarah tole you, so I stay still 'til she pass Nell down to me. Then I run 'roun the other side of the house and thas when the shots ring out. I hid in a bush 'til you was all running out on the lawn.'

'And you gave the baby back to Sarah.'

'Yes, missus,' she said. 'She call to me, then I run back to the kitchen and lock myself in with Rose 'til you come.'

'Where do you think Sarah might have gone?' I asked, though I didn't expect an honest answer. Delphine hung her head. 'I don' have no notion, missus,' she said.

'No matter,' I said confidently. 'She won't get far. If she hasn't returned within the week I shall take out a notice in the journals, and that will bring the slave-catchers like flies to sugar.'

Delphine made no response. I considered the last information as good as delivered to Sarah's ear. 'Send Rose to me,' I said. 'She'll have to serve upstairs until Sarah is returned.'

~

My father would never keep a runaway, but he never let one stay away either. If it took him six months and cost as much as the man was worth, he would gladly take the loss for the example it set the others to see a malcontent returned in shackles and straightway sold at market. He made sure all our negroes were informed of the proviso to the warranty, that whoever bought the man must know he had run away and could not be trusted, and that his value had been accordingly diminished. This policy resulted in a very low rate of absentees from our farm. Father deplored the laxity of his neighbors, who allowed a hand to disappear for two or three days at a time, always when the crop was in an urgent condition, then return to take his lashes and rejoin his companions with tales of his cleverness in eluding capture. Father wept with laughter when relating to us the policy of Mr Hampton of Lafourche Parish, who administered a certain

139

number of lashes for each day the slave went missing: fifteen for one day, thirty for two, etc. Father called this plan 'the three-day furlough,' for it was revealed that most of Mr Hampton's regular runaways returned by midnight of the third day, which this gentleman cited as proof of the efficacy of his system.

House servants were another matter. I can remember only one instance of a runaway from our house. It happened just after the fearful insurrection downriver when I was a girl. We were never in any danger from it, but Father went to the city just afterward and on his return told us what an alarming state the countryside was in. Five hundred slaves had simply gone mad and marched down the river road toward New Orleans, banging drums and waving flags. They killed Major Andry's son and wounded the major himself, set fire to mills and barns, raided the biggest houses. A stream of planters' families in wagons and carts, having taken flight in whatever vehicle they could quickly find, preceded the rebels into town.

It took almost ten days to rout the negroes. The governor called out the militia and every patrol in fifty miles. It cost the state so much the treasury was bankrupted, and the reimbursements had to be paid in installments. Father told Mother, when he thought I was asleep, though I was listening breathlessly on the landing, that the heads of the leaders were strung up in the trees all along the river from New Orleans to Major Andry's plantation, and many a planter took his negroes out to see this display.

That was when our housemaid Celeste disappeared. Father went back to the city and made inquiries until he learned that she had a brother among the insurrectionists. He was in fact one of the leaders. Father took a room in the hotel and spent several days following every rumor he could scare up. In the end he found Celeste hiding out in the restaurant kitchen where her mother worked as a cook. 'You have comforted one another mightily,' Father told her, 'but now it is time to come home.' She did not resist, returned to our house and stayed with us, always useful and even-tempered, until Father died.

I doubted that Sarah would be so tractable on her return. And if she made me spend much time or money tracking her down, I would not be so lenient.

$\sim$

How was I to remember exactly what she was wearing? I was running for my life. Sarah's costume didn't present itself as a remarkable feature of the evening. 'She had three dresses,' I told my aunt. 'One very like the other. What does it matter?'

'Well, it would help,' my aunt said, with a testiness that suggested she was wearying of my difficulties, though not so much as I. 'It is usually included.'

I closed my eyes and tried to recall the sleeve which I had clutched, endeavoring to stop her, the skirt rising in two puffs over the saddle as she rode away. 'It must have been the brown linsey,' I said. 'And she had the baby wrapped in her shawl, indigo wool; it was an old one of Mother's.'

'Very well,' my aunt said, bending over the page on which

141

she was writing out the notice. 'That will have to do.'

Aunt Lelia was convinced that Sarah was in the city, though my husband's horse had been found wandering on the levee a few miles north of here. 'She probably rode up to the landing at Bayou Sara, spent the night in hiding, and got on the ferry the next morning. She wouldn't have been so foolish as to ride south into the fracas. She will need money if she hopes to get anywhere, and she will doubtless call on Mr Roget for help.'

'Perhaps he has already provided for her,' I said. 'She had half a dozen opportunities to spin out a scheme with him when Mother was ill.'

But my aunt remained convinced that Sarah would not leave the area without meeting Mr Roget. 'She will try to pass for a free negro,' she said. 'With her color, she can easily bring it off.'

'Are you putting that in the notice?' I asked.

'Yes,' she said.

There were moments when I thought Sarah had plotted the entire insurrection, she and Mr Roget whispering together under my mother's house, though that was surely unlikely. She would not have been as frightened as she was, nor taken the precaution of getting her baby outside the house at the start. She only took advantage of the confusion, and of that event she must have longed for, my husband's death. She assumed I would be murdered as well and it would be several days before anyone would think to look for her. 'Number the slaves at the master's funeral,' my uncle is fond of saying. 'There is always one who will bolt.'

'I think this will do,' my aunt said, blotting her page. 'Shall I read it to you?'

'I suppose so,' I said.

'"Seventy-five dollars reward,"' she read.

'Isn't that rather high?' I asked.

'No, I think not. I have seen rewards as high as one hundred dollars for a house servant. They are often difficult to apprehend.'

'Go on,' I said.

'"The girl, Sarah, about twenty-seven years old, and her eight-month-old baby girl, called Nell, ran away October 27 from R. P. Gaudet plantation in Ascension Parish, tall, slender, fine-featured, light complexion, speaks English and some French, wearing brown linsey dress, indigo woolen shawl, no shoes, very likely, has scar behind left ear . . ."'

'I didn't know that,' I said.

'She fell into a fence when she was small,' my aunt said. 'It was mentioned in the title.' She continued her reading. '"Well spoken, of good address."'

'I wouldn't say so,' I said. 'I would say she was of sullen address.'

My aunt gave me a long look. 'She will be trying to get on,' she said. '"Will probably make her way to New Orleans, may pass as a free negro, fifty-dollar additional reward on proof to conviction of any person who may harbor her."'

'Won't that last bit just encourage Mr. Roget to send her out of town?'

'She won't stay with him,' my aunt replied. 'That would be too obvious.'

'Perhaps you're right,' I said, feeling thoroughly bored and aggravated by the whole business. My shoulder felt as though a hot iron were pressed against it and my head ached. 'Is it time for my medicine yet?'

My aunt put the page aside and came to my bed. 'My poor dear,' she said. 'Are you in great pain?'

'I am,' I said.

She poured out a spoonful of the sleeping tincture. 'Take this,' she said, 'and rest a bit. I'll go down and speak with Charles. He has brought his own driver over from Chatterly to serve as overseer here until you are well enough to decide what you want to do.'

I swallowed the medicine. 'I know what I want to do,' I said. 'I want to sell it all, everything and everyone.'

'We'll talk about it when you are strong again,' my aunt said, soothing me as she might a sickly child.

My head seemed to droop forward like a flower broken on its stalk. 'I fear I will never be strong again,' I said.

⌒

Dr Landry visited regularly to change the dressing on my shoulder and bring me news of the world. One morning he removed the bandages from my cheek and pulled the last stitches from my lip. 'The redness will fade,' he said, when I requested the looking glass. 'That gash in your cheek was so crooked it was the devil to sew.'

I gazed at my reflection. 'Now this is pitiful,' I said, pressing the swollen ridge that divided my lower lip. In truth it was not so bad as I had feared.

'A beautiful woman is rendered more beautiful by a scar,' Dr Landry opined. 'It reminds a man of what suffering she has endured. In your case, we are all awed by your courage.'

'The courage to run away and hide?'

'Many a woman would not have had it.'

I wondered if this were true. I remembered my state that night as one of general terror, punctuated by a few moments of clarity when I knew what to do. If that was courage, what good was it? Sarah, who had been terrified, was the one to ride away unharmed, and my husband, who even I could not deny had been brave, was dead. I was not so hypocritical as to be disturbed by the grim satisfaction I felt whenever that last fact surfaced in my consciousness. He was dead. He would be receiving no more reports. I smiled wanly at my altered reflection. It is worth it, I thought, handing the mirror back to Dr Landry. 'My husband saved my life,' I said honestly enough. The good doctor laid his hand upon my own and expressed again his deep sympathy for my loss.

Later, with his assistance, I was able to go downstairs for the first time. My aunt had put everything in order, but there was ample evidence of violence. The spyglass was dismantled and lay in pieces on the carpet, there were the gashes in the dining table, a curtain down, a mirror shattered so that only glass splinters remained in the frame. In my husband's office there were shot holes in the wall just inside the door. 'He fired and missed,' I observed to the doctor. 'Then somehow he got out alive, but he left his second pistol behind.'

'Unspeakable,' Dr Landry said. A weakness in my legs

caused me to lean hard upon his arm, and he led me to the chair, where I sank down gratefully. We heard a sound in the hall, a door slammed, there were quick footsteps coming toward us. Of course, I thought. I would not get off with just a few scars, a useless arm. My husband would have his revenge upon me, and he would have it every day for the rest of my life. Dr Landry looked out the door, his brow furrowed as a low whine began. He stepped aside, allowing the creature to pass into the room.

Delphine had cleaned him up and dressed him in short pants and a loose linen shirt half tucked in at the back. His face was still swollen, the bruise had faded to yellow. He came to my chair and began patting my knee, babbling nonsense with the confidence and intensity of a lawyer making an irresistible argument. I looked over his head at Dr Landry, who covered his beard with his hand and shook his head slowly. 'The heir apparent,' I said, and then, as if he understood me, Walter turned to the doctor and gave a shout of what sounded like joy.

~

I have never liked my husband's brother, Charles Gaudet. He's an arrogant man, boorish and supercilious, like my husband, only worse because he has been successful. He is the youngest of three brothers and the richest of all. Since my husband's murder, he has taken to strolling around this property as if he owned it, addressing me in solicitous tones, as if I were addled and must have every word repeated. As soon as I was well enough to receive a visitor, he was at the door, eager to get at my husband's books to see what chance he had of being repaid the money he was fool enough to loan his brother.

Rose was so poor at dressing my hair, I had her brush it out so it fell over my shoulders. I'd disguised my lip with rouge, my cheek with powder, and fixed my elbow so that it rested on the arm of the chair, thereby lifting my shoulder to a normal position. My recovery had left me thin and pale; the pallor intensified the blue of my eyes, or so I told myself. Charles's eyes betrayed only the mildest alarm when he came into the parlor, where I had arranged myself to receive him. I held out my left hand as he approached and he bent over it, brushing his lips against the bridge of my fingers. 'My dearest sister,' he said. 'You have been in my prayers every minute.'

'Do you pray so often?' I said.

He stepped back, remembering that I had never been charmed by him. He tried another line. 'Maybelle sends her love and her sympathy,' he said.

Then I felt sorry for him, because Maybelle is as fat as a hog. That thought led straight to a pang of guilt. Maybelle alone of my relatives showed me the courtesy of refraining from any mention of God in her condolence letter at Mother's death. She recounted a kindness Mother had done for her when her son was ill and Mother directed her to a specialist. Everyone else felt the need to assure me that Mother's death was part of God's plan. Exactly, I wanted to shout after reading this sentiment half a dozen times – his plan is to kill us all, and if an innocent child dies in agony and a wicked man breathes his last at an advanced age in his sleep, who are we to call it injustice?

'Please give Maybelle my warmest regards,' I said to Charles.

He wandered away to a chair and lowered himself into it with the care of a man who has been riding all day. 'Your aunt tells me that you are feeling well enough to take an interest in your affairs.'

'I am,' I said. 'It seems to me there's a great deal to attend to.'

'You needn't be bothered with any of it,' he said. 'We are in hopes that you will come to live with us at Chatterly.'

My aunt has told him what Mother's estate is worth, I thought. 'That is kind,' I said. 'But I long to be near my aunt, to be of use to her. She has been so good to me.'

'I see,' he said. 'The children will be disappointed.'

This remark was shockingly transparent, as I hardly knew my nieces and nephew, nor have they ever expressed the slightest interest in my acquaintance. I looked about the room, resting my eyes upon various empty spaces where ghosts might reside, and indeed I felt a curious chill, such as I used to experience when my husband looked at me. 'I can't bear being in the country, Charles,' I said. 'I never feel safe for one minute.'

'Of course,' he said. 'I hadn't thought of that.'

'I want to sell this place and everyone in it, except Delphine.'

'I'm sure a buyer could be found,' he said. 'But I fear the price will not be satisfactory.'

'My husband was in debt to half the parish,' I said, enjoying the amazement that settled upon my counselor.

148

'He owed you five thousand dollars, isn't that correct? Close to six with interest.'

'I'm not sure of the exact amount.'

'He owed the banks a fortune, he owes the factor more than he would have made on this year's crop. Still, I think if I sell everything, even at a poor price, it will clear out the debt.'

'I would have to look into his books,' he offered, but tentatively now.

'Yes, you should do that,' I said. 'You might want to take a glass of whiskey with you, to brace yourself against the shock.'

'My poor brother,' he said, considering the full extent of my husband's folly, which included having a wife who knew what he was worth.

'Fortunately, I have my mother's estate,' I said. 'I will move into her house in town. The income from her investments will be sufficient for my needs, so I should have no occasion to call upon the charity of my husband's relatives.'

He frowned. 'I am pleased to learn that you will be independent,' he said. 'I think you couldn't be at peace any other way. But it is wrong for you to speak of the solemn obligation I bear my brother's widow as charity. If you were penniless, I would consider it both my duty and an honor to provide for you.'

It was the first time anyone had called me a widow to my face. I liked the sound of it. I pictured my fate in this man's house if I were forced to rely upon his honor – the widowed aunt, sulking about with an embroidery hoop, called upon to play the piano when the young people wanted

149

to dance – and I sent a heartfelt message of gratitude to my mother for her sound investments, her excellent financial sense.

'Thank you, Charles,' I said. 'May I rely upon you to see to the sale?'

'I will speak to my agent today.' He looked about the room, valuing the furniture with what I suspected was an expert eye. 'He will want to make an inventory.'

'I'll take a few small pieces,' I said. 'The dresser and carpet in my bedroom. Delphine will doubtless want some indispensable pot or spoon.'

'Of course,' he said.

'If there is anything you want for yourself, or that Maybelle might want, please feel free . . .'

'No,' he said. 'That would not be correct, unless I deduct the value from my poor brother's debt.'

'At least take his pistols,' I said. 'He would want them to stay in the family.'

His eyes settled upon me, full of sentiment. 'A thoughtful suggestion,' he said. 'I will take them with pleasure.'

My shoulder had begun to ache and I longed to terminate the interview, yet I couldn't resist one final test of my relative's goodwill. 'I don't suppose you would be willing to take Walter off my hands,' I said.

His cheeks flushed and he gave a nervous cough. It was with difficulty that I maintained a frank, interested expression. 'Manon . . .' he said, searching for words. This was one piece of his brother's property he wanted nothing to do with. I pictured Walter running across the veranda at Chatterly to greet the guests at the annual ball. 'My little nephew,' Charles might explain, while Walter rubbed mud into some elegant gentleman's waistcoat. 'Maybelle . . .' Charles continued. 'She hasn't been well . . .'

'It's all right, Charles,' I said, taking pity on him. 'You've no obligation to take him. Delphine is the only one who can manage him and for some reason she's attached to him.'

'Then it would be for the best . . .' he stammered.

'It would be for the best if that child had never been born,' I said.

My brother-in-law nodded sagely. 'I understand the mother has run away.'

'She has,' I said. 'But I expect we will find her soon. Don't put her name on the inventory. I don't plan to sell her.'

He gave me a questioning look. I could no longer bear the pain in my shoulder. I eased my elbow from its support and winced as my arm fell limp across my lap. 'If I have to live with Walter,' I said, 'so does she.'

PART FOUR

~

En Ville

'Your uncle is persuaded that we should engage Mr Leggett,' my aunt said. We were seated in the parlor of my cottage. It had taken me barely three weeks to be resettled in this agreeable domicile. My aunt was eager to return to town, and, as I couldn't be expected to spend a night alone in my husband's house, I had come down with her, leaving Rose and Delphine to pack my clothes and follow. I was propped up on pillows on the settee, and my aunt had turned the chair of Mother's desk to face me. It was chilly outside, but we had a fire in the grate, the curtains drawn, the lamps lit.

'How could she have disappeared so completely?' I said.

'Your uncle believes she is no longer in town. His inquiries usually result in some leads, but in this case he has come up with nothing.'

'I assume Mr Roget has been interviewed.'

'Repeatedly, though not by your uncle. They are not on speaking terms.'

'Is Mr Leggett a trustworthy person?'

My aunt sent a dismissive puff of air through her nostrils. 'None of them are trustworthy,' she said. 'They are the worst sort of men. They inflate their expenses past all reason and there's nothing to be done about it. But your uncle has employed Mr Leggett in the past with some success. He will want twenty-five dollars in advance, against the reward.'

'And if he fails to bring her back?'

'The money is forfeit,' she explained. 'There is no guarantee that he will find her. He is complaining that we have allowed too much time to pass. If she is, as your uncle suspects, making her way north, she may have gotten quite far by now. Mr Leggett has retrieved runaways from as far away as Boston, but it takes time. Once she is in a free state, he can't rely on cooperation from the authorities, though there are always those who will assist in a capture for a price.'

'Boston!' I said.

'It does seem unlikely,' my aunt agreed. 'Mr Leggett wants to know if she has any relatives in the North who might assist her.'

'Not that I know of,' I said. 'She never spoke of anyone. Do you know where she was born?'

'Mississippi, I believe. She was from a plantation near Natchez. I assume that's where she was born.'

'Perhaps she has gone there.'

'I think not,' my aunt said. 'She was sold as part of a bankruptcy settlement.'

'Is that where Uncle Emile bought her?'

156

'No. He bought her from a sugar planter in St John Parish. Actually, he took her in payment of a debt. He knew I was in need of a housekeeper. She was just fifteen or sixteen, very bright and willing, though she had a stubborn streak even then.'

'She is stubborn,' I mused.

'I still believe Mr Roget knows where she is.'

I recalled my one sighting of Mr Roget as he turned from Sarah, lifting his hat to me and walking away. 'She told me she had a brother,' I said. 'I didn't believe it at the time, but perhaps it is true. She said Mr Roget came here to give her the message that her brother had been leased to work on the docks.'

'Did she say the brother's name?'

'Clarence,' I said. 'But why would she tell me if she planned to escape with his help?'

'Perhaps she had not yet formulated the plan.'

'Could she have boarded an ocean vessel?'

'If she were in disguise, if she had money and passed as a free negro? I think it entirely possible.'

'But she speaks so poorly. Surely someone would notice.'

'Sometimes the dullest negro is discovered to have a perfectly good wit when it serves his purpose. And she might not be called upon to speak very much.'

I imagined Sarah, dressed in some borrowed finery, her hair pulled up in a good bonnet, her elbows propped on the rail of a ship, while the water churned below her and the miles between her and the world she knew slipped away.

'You are right,' I told my aunt. 'We must tell Mr Leggett

about this brother and bid him make inquiries on the docks.'

~

Joel Borden sent flowers on the day I arrived, and again a week later, this time with a note asking if he might visit me. I examined my face in the mirror. The swelling and redness were largely gone, and a normal color had returned to my complexion. My shoulder ached, especially as the weather turned cooler, but the wound was closed over. I kept only a thin bandage on it to keep the cloth of my dress from rubbing against it. Yes, I decided, I would see him. I sent Rose with an answer, suggesting four the following afternoon as the hour for our tête-à-tête.

As that hour approached, I was giddy with excitement, a condition completely inappropriate for one so recently widowed. I had Rose take Walter out to the levee with strict orders to stay away from the house for several hours. Rose liked nothing better than strolling about the town with the poor idiot on a halter and leash that Delphine had fashioned for him. I had Delphine move an armchair close to the settee and put the coffee urn on a table in reach of my good arm. Then I waited for the bell, which sounded promptly at four. Delphine passed through the room to admit Joel, then scurried back to the kitchen while he stood in the parlor doorway smiling down at me. 'At last,' he said. 'I have tried to be patient until you were well enough to receive visitors, but I have not had an easy moment until this one.'

'I fear you will find me sadly changed,' I said.

He came in and took the chair near me, leaning forward to look into my face. 'After what you have been through,' he said, 'how could you not be changed?' There was no trace of revulsion in his scrutiny, only a fascinated admiration, such as I had seen in my uncle's eyes when he visited. I had survived that which we all in some degree feared. 'Your aunt told me that you spent the entire night hiding in the forest, wounded by a gunshot.'

I lifted my useless arm by the wrist and let it fall back into my lap. 'This is the result,' I said.

'My dear,' he said.

'I try not to think about any of it.'

He sat back in his chair. 'You are right. You must go on with your life.' He looked around the room at the fire, the paintings, the vase of flowers on the side table. 'What a comfort it must be to you to be back in this house.'

'It is,' I said. 'It makes me think of happier times.' I turned to the coffee urn. 'Will you have coffee? Or would you prefer a glass of sherry?'

'Let me serve you,' he said, getting up. He busied himself with the cups and saucers, pouring the coffee and milk together expertly and talking all the while. 'I have visited your aunt regularly to keep up with your progress. She tells me your brother-in-law is handling the sale of your plantation and that an American has offered to buy it outright with everything in it.'

'Mr Kenilworth,' I said. 'He has come out of the North like a god, possessed of more money than sense and a fantasy about being a planter that I've no doubt will rob him of both.'

'Poor Mr Kenilworth.' Joel chuckled, handing me my cup. 'You know, I'm never certain if it is your wit or your beauty that pleases me most.'

'You are easily pleased,' I said. 'Perhaps as easily as Mr Kenilworth.'

'I care nothing for him,' Joel said, 'but that he serve the purpose of making you rich.'

'Alas, I fear that's something even Mr Kenilworth cannot do.'

Joel resumed his seat, and stirred his coffee, looking puzzled.

'My husband was heavily in debt,' I explained. 'Mr Kenilworth's offer will barely cancel it.'

'I didn't know,' Joel said somberly, as if he'd just heard of the death of a favorite dog. He looked up, then back down. For the first time in my memory, he was at a loss for words. All this time he has been thinking I would be rich, I thought. For a moment we sat silently, staring into the reality of his requirements and my resources.

'Fortunately,' I said, 'Mother's estate is adequate. I'm not rich, but I am independent.'

'And well out of sugar,' Joel responded, rousing himself. 'I'm sorry to hear that your husband was unsuccessful, but he was certainly not alone in that.'

'Do you never think of quitting it yourself?'

'I should,' he said. 'I hate it. I never go to Rivière. But I'm continually advised to wait, as the economic tide will turn, or the weather change, or the negroes all get well by some miracle and start doing a decent day's work. What else can I do? I'm not fit for business. Half the time I live on credit from my factor.' He sipped his coffee, resting his eyes on the portrait of my father, whom he never met. 'It seems the happiest years are behind us,' he said.

I set my cup on the side table and leaned back into the cushions, seeking to ease the pain in my shoulder. 'I've never known you to be melancholy,' I said. 'I was counting on you to cheer me up.'

Joel opened his eyes wide, as if he'd just glanced at his reflection and seen someone he didn't recognize. 'As you have every right to expect,' he said. 'You must forgive me.'

'I do,' I said. And I did, but the effort fatigued me. It seemed that happiness must always be just beyond me and I should always stand gazing in at it as through a shop-window where everything glittered and appealed to me, but I had not enough money to enter. It was money, only money, that would keep Joel from ever being more than my friendly admirer.

Joel struggled to rise above the somber mood that had fallen upon us. 'I have some excellent gossip for you,' he said. 'Pierre Legrand has finally gotten his comeuppance.' He launched into an amusing story about a man we both despised whose wife had discovered his craven efforts to seduce her niece. After that he went on to another hilarious account of a distinguished lady who had proved a poor loser at bezique. 'You are a tonic,' I said, when I had paused from laughing. 'And I must pay for my medicine. May I offer you some champagne?'

'It is what the doctor recommends,' he exclaimed.

'Ring for Delphine,' I said, and he rose to pull the cord. She came in, wiping her hands on her apron, her chin tucked nearly into her breastbone. I gave her my instructions – there were oysters as well; I'd had Rose buy them in the morning – and she went out hurriedly. 'She's not accustomed to serving,' I said. 'She is mortified to leave the kitchen.'

'What's become of Peek?' he inquired.

'I had to give her away. She was getting on and her cooking really is abominable. Delphine is an accomplished cook. In a few weeks I will give a small dinner party and you may sample her daube.'

'Gladly,' he agreed. Delphine came in, desperately clutching a tray, in terror that the glasses must tumble over. Joel directed her to the desk, clearing away the few papers scattered over it. 'Well done,' he said, as she backed away. 'No need to stay. I'll serve your mistress with pleasure.' She hurried out, casting me a cautious look, but I waved her away. Joel struggled with the cork, then there was the sharp pop that is the signifier of gaiety. He turned to me, holding the bottle close over a crystal flute as the golden liquid frothed inside. His eyes were bright, his smile infectious. He was turning his own pleasure over in his mind. My mother had offered maternal kindness, boundless admiration, and the occasional dinner. My tenure would be more enticing. He handed me a glass, filled one for himself, and proposed a toast. 'To this house,' he said, 'which is for me the sweetest refuge in the civilized world.'

162

It wasn't long before the bottle was empty and the refuge, at least for one evening, no longer requisite. There was a dinner engagement and after that gambling or dancing; a city full of amusements to tempt my guest from my cozy parlor. At the door Joel took my hands and gave me a brotherly kiss on each cheek. 'I am dining at your aunt's on Saturday,' he said. 'Will you be there?'

'I will make a point of it,' I said. Then he went out into the street.

I bolted the door and leaned against the wall, light-headed but not lighthearted; in fact a considerable darkness descended upon me. I went back to the settee and sat gazing into the fire.

Standing in the doorway, bidding Joel good-night, had made me think of my husband, of his visits in this house so long ago, when I was too naïve to understand the nature of the bargain I was making. I was young, I was pretty, and I had no money. My husband was of a good family, had expectations and a large house. I didn't find him particularly attractive, but I felt no positive revulsion, and I enjoyed how strongly he seemed to be attracted to me. His eyes were always moving over me. If I let him touch my hand or my waist, I could feel his struggle to refrain from pulling me to him. Mother observed this and, as it didn't disturb her, I took it to be in the proper order of things. 'Mr Gaudet is taken with you,' she said. 'I think we needn't worry too much about the dowry.' I had in myself, I concluded, some value, something more desirable to my husband than money. At the time, this struck me as unusual.

My invincible stupidity was revealed to me on my wedding night. My mother's house having been reckoned too small, when the wedding celebrations were over I was arranged upon the bed in a room at my aunt's house. The servant was sent away; my husband came in unfastening his cuffs. He pushed the door closed with his boot. Mother's entire advice had been the word 'submit,' but I had no more idea of what I would be submitting to than I had of the workings of a steam engine. A likely metaphor! My husband roared over me like a locomotive. There were moments when it seemed to me his object was to pull my limbs from their joints. I glanced over his shoulder at the mantel clock, anxious to know how long the operation might take. My breasts, which had never been touched by another, save a servant with a sponge, were so kneaded and sucked upon I feared they would be blackened by bruises. I wanted to shout to my mother, 'Why did you not warn me?' but then it occurred to me that Father would never have subjected another creature to such an assualt. I looked into my husband's reddened face, at his eyes, which seemed to start from their sockets, at his lips swollen by his passion. Was there to be no trace of feeling for my helplessness, no tenderness in my marital bed? The answer to both these questions was no, none. Afterward he was silent, not critical, there were no harsh words. He did not appear to be displeased. He had exhausted himself and within a few minutes was sound asleep. I touched the damp sheet beneath my hips and found my fingertips reddened with blood. I am married, I thought, looking at his sleeping face. His mouth was open, his breathing as easy and peaceful as a child's. This is my husband, I thought.

We stayed in town for two weeks. I was given to understand by my aunt and my mother that these would be the happiest days of my marriage. That turned out to be true. I was not unhappy. There was the novelty of being greeted by friends who clearly thought I'd done well for myself. My husband had not yet begun his long descent into bankruptcy, so there was money to spend. We gave a dinner at the hotel which was heralded in the journals as one of the most delightful of the season.

The fury of my husband's nightly assaults did not abate, but they interested me, and I soon discovered I was strong enough to withstand him. I persisted in the delusion that the intensity of his abandonment was the direct result of some power I had over him, which must somehow accrue to my benefit. I went so far as to anticipate his pleasure, I encouraged him, and found some pleasure in it. I entered the fray. Later, when I understood that my sense of having some particular value to him was a delusion, this willingness on my part became a source of deep humiliation.

I found our conversations more trying than those hours we spent in what passed for conjugal embracing. My husband could talk about sugar, he was knowledgeable about wine and spirits, he liked to shoot animals; this was the range of his interests. Art and music meant nothing to him; he could not concentrate on a picture long enough to see it. Five minutes of my performance upon a piano put him into a deep sleep. Whenever he spoke in company, I noticed the other young men politely waiting for him to finish so that the subject could be changed. When their repartee became sprightly, he looked from one to the other with a dumbfounded expression. He rarely laughed.

That he was dull, that he was without tenderness: was this reason enough to hate him? Surely not, but by the time we left the city, I had come to dread the feelings that must arise in my own breast when I was dependent on my husband alone for whatever joy life might have left to offer me. And I was right to be afraid. In town he was unsure of himself, but in his own home he was a tyrant. He drained the color from every scene, the flavor from every bit of food, the warmth from every exchange of sentiment. He had not so much destroyed my life as emptied it, and now that he was gone, I had to pretend there was something alive in me. Joel had sensed this. My laughter was too ready, and it was hollow. When he looked into my eyes, it must have been like staring through the windows of a burnt-out house. Doubtless, he attributed this to the ordeal of the insurrection, and it didn't occur to him that what had left me with ashes for a heart was not murderous negroes, but my marriage.

The coals had crumbled in the grate and a chill rose up from beneath my feet. Images from the night I wanted to forget flickered across my mind: the horse champing the grass, the sharp blow to my jaw, the flare of the torch, Sarah pausing to point into the darkness, my husband's startled face as his murderer pulled him up by his hair. I examined his expression as if I were looking at a painting, and I discovered a detail I hadn't noticed before. The moment before the fatal blow was struck, my husband called Sarah's name.

I heard the gate open, the sound of footsteps in the alley: Rose and Walter returning from their excursion. There was the repeated slapping of a hand against the side of the house, all the way to the back. Walter, I thought. My husband's curse, as impossible to accustom myself to or rid myself of as my own crippled right arm.

~

'How can a light woman and a dark child disappear without a trace?' I complained to my aunt. We were seated in her drawing room. On the table between us lay a much-crumpled, atrociously written letter, the report of Mr Leggett on his efforts to secure the runaway Sarah.

'He has been up the coast as far as Savannah,' my aunt said, 'quizzing the captains and the stewards of every ship.'

'Has he located the brother?'

'I'm afraid not,' my aunt said.

I bent over the offensive scrawl, trying to make out a sentence. *Captain Wash ceen only won child as caut.* 'What does this mean?' I exclaimed.

My aunt examined the sentence. 'Mr Leggett takes an original approach to spelling and punctuation,' she observed.

'It's appalling.'

'Yes. It is, isn't it? It took me some time to make any sense of it at all. Your uncle is nearly an adept. He was able to give me a summary within twenty minutes of first viewing the document.'

'What must his speech be like?' I said.

'Not much less recondite, I'm afraid. However, he's good at figures. He can compose an excellent invoice.'

'That doesn't surprise me,' I said.

'No,' she agreed. 'What he says is that a Captain Wash, that's probably Walsh, your uncle thinks, has seen only one such dark baby girl in the last month, and it was in the company of its mother, equally dark, a servant traveling with her owner, who was an elderly white gentleman en route to visit his doctor in Philadelphia.'

'Well, that is certainly useless information.'

'There were no free women of color on that trip. Might she have separated from the child?'

'It was weaned. It's possible.'

My aunt turned the page over, skimming the lines. 'Mr Leggett did find a report of two free women, sisters, traveling together, about the right age, but he traced them to St Louis and found they were well known in their neighborhood.'

'Perhaps she is disguised as a servant and some northerner is playing her master.'

'Or she may not be traveling by boat, or she somehow contrived to blend in with the other passengers, or she is still here among us, but we just don't see her,' my aunt said. 'There's no way of knowing.'

'No,' I agreed. 'Should we increase the reward?'

'I think so,' my aunt said. 'And we'd best insert the notice in the papers in a few of the larger towns.'

'Very well,' I said.

'I don't despair of Mr Leggett's finding her,' my aunt assured me. 'He has a marvelous persistence.'

'So has she,' I said.

When I left my aunt's, I walked to the Faubourg Marigny to leave a pair of shoes with the shoemaker there. That neighborhood is populated largely by free negroes, and a more arrogant and supercilious group could hardly be found. As I went among them, I found myself turning again and again to follow a figure or face that resembled Sarah's. A man in a bright yellow frock coat approached me, his eyes meeting mine with perfect insolence, and for a moment I thought it must be Mr Roget, though I had had such a brief glimpse of this person it was unlikely that I would recognize him. Was Sarah in hiding behind one of these simple house-fronts? Was Mr Roget even now writing to her with further instructions for their eventual reunion?

The shoemaker, Mr Gaston, an elderly man rumored to be related to the police chief, came out from behind his counter to offer his condolences for my recent losses. He had kept Mother in shoe soles for twenty years and had seen me often enough at her side when I was a girl. He was a tall, thin man, very light, with black eyes and thick curly white hair he kept cropped close to his skull. As I thanked him for his kind words, he lowered his eyes, then raised them again, and with a slow smile inquired how he might be of service to me. Something in his manner, perhaps it was only the irritating lack of deference, reminded me of Sarah. We discussed my shoes and parted agreeably. When I was on the street, I thought of how he had lowered his eyes modestly, then the suddenness of his redirected gaze. I had come to the turn to my own house, but I passed it by and proceeded to Rue Chartres, where I turned south toward my aunt's residence. I walked quickly, pressed by the force of revelation, as well as a sense that time was of the essence. I was as certain of the facts as if I had read them in the journals. The dark baby Mr Leggett described was indeed Sarah's child, and she was traveling with her mother. But her mother was not the servant, who was an impostor, hired by Mr Roget to play a part. And the old gentleman en route to visit his doctor was neither seriously ill nor a gentleman. He was Sarah.

~

Mourning forbade my appearance at large gatherings, but a small dinner party of friends and family was not denied me. My aunt was anxious to alleviate my loneliness, and as my health returned, she insisted that I dine at her house two or three times a week. Often she invited another guest or two to fill out the table. Our family has been much decimated by the ravages of time. I have lost both my parents and two baby brothers; my aunt's two brothers both died before they were twenty and, of her three children, one son survived to adulthood, only to be killed in a hunting accident a week before his wedding day. My uncle's family fared little better, though he has several grown nephews and nieces and one brother, who lives in France. So we are all in all to each other. My childlessness had long been a source of vexation to my aunt; she had joined Mother in urging me to seek medical counsel, but as my husband was gone and I was not a marriageable commodity, I expected that she would resign herself and think of me as her last child. Yet she was so constituted that she couldn't give up all hope. One day, when she found me sitting in my darkened parlor with red-rimmed eyes, she opined that I should not despair; I was still young and beautiful; a suitor would materialize as soon as I returned to society. This was so unlikely, I told her, it was funny, and I thanked her for cheering me. Who would marry a cripple with only enough money to keep herself? Poor Aunt Lelia resorted to pointing out the promising rise in property values in our neighborhood.

I thought her surprisingly chilly to Joel Borden the following Saturday evening when we sat down to her dining table. I knew there was no hope of Joel's marrying me; he was desperate for money. That he behaved toward me as gallantly as any suitor was an irony I was prepared to accept, but I saw that it was not pleasing to my aunt. She had invited another gentleman, Mr Duffossat, a dull, myopic young man just finishing his law studies, who followed the banter between Joel and me with a furrowed brow. He was ponderous and overweight, showing signs of animation only at the presentation of dessert.

After supper we took our coffee to the dining room and sat down to a game of écarté. It was an unseasonably warm night and the balcony doors were open, the lamps dimly lit. From the street the sounds of talking, laughing, the clip-clop of horses' hooves, drifted up to us. My uncle did not play but occupied himself in standing behind my aunt's chair, supervising her game. Joel was in high spirits, impulsively raising the bid again and again. My aunt took a card

171

and sighed. Uncle Emile, resting his hand upon her shoulder, leaned down to whisper a word of advice into her ear. She smiled, adjusted her cards, then absently raised her hand to tap affectionately at his fingers. I looked away; it seemed such an intimate gesture I felt embarrassed to have seen it. My deflected gaze collided with Mr Duffossat's, which he redirected to his cards with a similar flustered haste. He had been closely observing the peculiarly lifeless slope of my right shoulder.

I felt a wave of heat rising from my neck and across my face. I glanced at Joel, who was speaking to my uncle about someone with an odd name, Balboa. Then I realized it was not a man, but a horse. My heart pounded in my ears and I was short of breath. I laid my cards facedown upon the table.

'Manon?' my aunt said. 'Are you feeling unwell?'

'It's so hot,' I said.

'I'll bring you some water,' my uncle said, turning to the sideboard.

Joel got to his feet and came to my side. 'Shall I help you to the chaise longue?' he said.

'She must rest in my room,' my aunt directed. 'It is cooler there.'

'I think I would like to lie down just for a few minutes,' I said, pushing back my chair. My aunt displaced Joel, who was left fretting as she guided me back through the dining room to her bedroom. As she had predicted, it was cooler, dark and quiet. I sank down on the bed and pulled off my shoes while she poured water into the washbasin, dropped a cloth into it, and carefully wrung it out. 'I don't know what's wrong with me,' I said, falling back upon the pillow.

'Your nerves are destroyed,' she said.

I smiled, thinking of my nerves. What were they, exactly? My aunt brought the cloth and laid it across my forehead. It was marvelously comforting. 'You must go back to your guests,' I said.

'They won't require me. Your uncle will take over my hand. He has been wanting to all evening.'

'Joel is betting recklessly,' I observed.

'As well he might,' my aunt said huffily. 'He is about to come into a great deal of money.'

How was this possible? Everyone knew Joel's father had gambled his fortune away. Had some distant relative remembered him? If Joel were rich . . . I hesitated to finish this proposition. It was as if I stood with my hand upon a doorknob, too timid to turn it and discover what might be on the other side, for, oh, what vistas might be there! 'What's happened?' I asked my aunt.

'He has proposed to Alice McKenzie and her father has accepted him, though not without serious reservations, as you can imagine.'

The imaginary door swung open and I found myself teetering at the brink of a black abyss. 'Oh,' I said.

'It was only settled yesterday, though they have been going back and forth for a month now.'

The McKenzies were a numerous family and a wealthy one. Their house in the American section was famously ostentatious. There were four or five sisters, several boys. The mother was known to admire Creole society. 'How old is Alice?' I asked.

'Not a girl,' my aunt said. 'She may be twenty-five. She's rather plain, I'm told, and of course she has no manners.'

It was bound to happen, I told myself. Joel couldn't go on indefinitely without money. 'Where will they live?'

'That's not settled. John McKenzie has an *envie* to make something of Rivière, the mother wants Alice in a house in the Carré, if she can find one big enough, which isn't likely. Joel doesn't want to leave town, of course; he loathes the country.'

That's two of us, I thought. Joel's visits might be quite regular. A plain wife wouldn't object to his maintaining a friendship with an unfortunate widow. Yet this thought gave me no comfort. Joel married, I thought. I sighed and closed my eyes, wishing my aunt would leave me.

But she expanded upon her topic. 'Though if he insists on spending entire evenings at the gambling tables and the Blue Ribbon Balls,' she said, 'he may find his mother-in-law perfectly willing to pack him off to Rivière for the rest of his days. I think John McKenzie unlikely to tolerate the expense of a little house on the Ramparts.'

'That's absurd,' I said. 'Joel would never do such a thing.'

My aunt gave me an indulgent smile. 'You are an innocent,' she said.

'I can't bear to hear another word,' I complained.

'No,' my aunt said. 'It's better that you don't. I'll leave you to rest. When you are ready, your uncle will walk you home.' Then she went out, leaving the door ajar so that the light from the hall lamp made a flickering band across the carpet.

Was it true? I thought. Did Joel spend his evenings at

those obscene dances where the women were all light-skinned courtesans whose mothers sat fanning themselves in the shadows and anticipating offers? Would he, as my aunt believed, set up one of these dreadful quadroons in a house of her own and use his wife's fortune to provide for whatever children she might bear him? It wasn't possible. Joel never looked at the servants; he hardly noticed they were there.

I had seen one of these women once, when Mother and I were visiting a neighbor, Mrs Perot. We were sitting in her drawing room drinking coffee and talking about wall covering when there was a ruckus at the door, a woman shouting. Mrs Perot's servant rushed in, disclaiming any power to forestall the advance of the visitor, who was hard on her heels. The woman stopped at the doorway, looking from one of us to the other, uncertain which to address. It could not be denied that she was an impressive figure. Her features were fine, though her lips were too thick, and her posture erect. She was dressed to perfection in the latest fashion: a morning dress of pale lavender silk with deep purple velvet edging at the sleeves and throat, and a satin bonnet of the same dark hue edged in black. She was in a state of great agitation. Her black eyes settled on our hostess, who rose from her chair with admirable calm and said, 'May I help you in some way?'

'It's I who will help you, madame,' she said, 'if you wish your husband murdered.'

'Please excuse me,' our hostess said to us, advancing upon her visitor. 'Will you come with me?' she said, going out into the hall.

The woman cast us an angry glance, then followed her quarry, denouncing her. She lapsed into French, threatening more dire consequences at every step; the burning down of Mr Perot's place of business, the murder of her own children, the death of Mrs Perot's young sons, whom she knew by name. Our hostess called for her butler, who appeared at once, throwing open the front door and forcefully escorting the enraged woman out into the street.

Mother turned to me and said softly, 'Mr Perot has at last acceded to his wife's wishes.' In a moment our hostess returned and we continued our conversation.

What struck me most about the horrible creature was her excellent French. That perfect accent coming out of that yellow face, those dark eyes flashing with rage, made her seem like a grotesque doll, created as some sort of poor joke, which I suppose is exactly what she was, what they all are.

I lay in my aunt's bed, sick with the recollection of this vengeful madwoman and the thought that Joel enjoyed the company of others like her, that he might one evening leave my little house and rush to another even smaller, where he was the master, yet no guest ever came. From the hall the voices of the cardplayers drifted in. If I listened closely I could pick out from the general ripple of gaiety the deep tremor of Joel's laughter. With a shudder of misery I understood that I would never again feel aught but bitterness to hear it.

❧

After I had slept a little and the guests were gone, my uncle walked with me to my cottage. The night had grown cooler, and though it was late the streets were by no means deserted. Some of our neighbors sat out on their balconies, gentlemen mostly, smoking cigars and discussing cotton futures in groups of three or four. I took my uncle's arm as I had so often when I was a girl. 'We have had a new report from Mr Leggett,' he said.

'Has he found her?'

'Not yet,' he said. 'But it does appear that your suspicion that she has disguised herself may be correct. He has attempted to trace the gentleman traveling for his health and there is no evidence that such a person exists.'

'Where was she last seen?'

'If it is she,' my uncle cautioned. 'He can't be certain, of course. This gentleman was traveling under the name of Mr Claude Maître and he is known to have disembarked from the *United States* at Savannah. He hardly spoke to anyone on the trip, he kept to his berth, and the steward says he didn't sleep but sat up in his chair fully dressed. He never removed his hat.'

'That's because his long hair would fall down.'

My uncle smiled. 'It's remarkable, don't you think? How did you guess it?'

'I thought it odd that a sick man would travel with a woman and a baby. Why wouldn't he take a boy, who would be more useful?'

'It's so bold,' my uncle said. 'Here I have been imagining her hiding out in the swamps, perhaps meeting up with one of Murrel's men, who would pretend to be her

177

guide, and then sell her to Indians, and instead she has been traveling north in a private cabin.'

'She wouldn't be so bold if someone weren't helping her.'

'No. That's certainly true,' my uncle agreed. We did not say the name that sprang to both our lips because my uncle can hardly speak of Mr Roget without becoming agitated. 'Well, we shall see,' he concluded. 'Mr Leggett believes the Philadelphia destination is a ploy, and that she will more likely try to reach New York. Here we are,' he said, as we had arrived at my door. I bid him good-night and let myself into the parlor, where I sat in the dark for some time, entertaining the idea of Sarah passing as a sick white gentleman in the freezing metropolis of New York. Even if she were apprehended at once, it might be weeks before she was returned. I pulled a straying lock of hair back from my face; it might be best to send Rose out to study with a decent hairdresser. She was much improved as a housekeeper, and she managed Walter as well as Delphine did. She was presentable, willing, and she liked living in town. I had thought to sell her when Sarah returned, but it might be more practical to sell Sarah.

As I so mused, my eyes fell upon the side table, where I noticed a white card left on the salver. Joel, I thought. He must have stopped by on his way to his next party and written a line of courteous concern about my indisposition at my aunt's card table. Party? I asked myself, as I lit the lamp and reached for the card, or a room full of fancy yellow harlots?

But it wasn't his card. It was larger and the lettering

178

was different. I held it close to the light and read the
legend:

EVERETT ROGET
Tasteful and elegant carpentry
Interior and exterior painting and plaster
Faux marble and fresco

I turned it over and read the carefully lettered message on
the reverse:

Dear Mrs Gaudet,
I hope you will allow me to call upon you tomorrow
afternoon at two on a matter of import to us both.
Respectfully,
Everett Roget h.c.l.

～

After breakfast I consulted with my aunt, who agreed with
me that Mr Roget knew exactly where Sarah was and
intended to make an offer pending her return. 'He may
seem sure of himself,' she said. 'He has established some
means of contacting Sarah quickly and he thinks she is so
well hidden no one can find her. But he must know Mr
Leggett has been commissioned to apprehend her. This is
a desperate measure.'

Mr Roget did not appear in the least desperate when he
arrived at my door that afternoon. As he followed Rose into
the parlor his eyes darted confidently over the cornices, the

mantel, the baseboards, then settled upon me with much the same quality of appraisal and assurance. He was neatly dressed, though not elegant in any part, except for his walking stick, which had a silver knob. He took the seat I directed him to, set his hat upon the side table, and held the stick between his legs. His hands, I noticed, were large, chapped from the cold and the dry plaster of his trade, the nails neatly trimmed. One was bruised black at the quick. He was light-skinned, though not so light as Sarah, and his features were pleasing, especially his eyes, which were wide, dark brown, the lashes thick for a man. He began almost at once, offering his condolences for my recent losses and apologizing for having taken the liberty to disturb me in my mourning.

'It is for just that reason that I must ask you to come directly to the reason for your visit,' I said.

He compressed his lips in a tight, self-satisfied smile that suggested he had not expected to be treated courteously, and was now justified in that expectation. I leaned forward over the arm of my chair, giving him my close attention.

'I have come in hopes that you will accept an offer for the purchase of your servant Sarah.'

'Sarah?' I pretended surprise. 'But she is not for sale. Are you in the habit of offering to buy servants who are not for sale?'

He raised his eyes to mine. 'No,' he said.

'Then I wonder what has driven you to such impertinence in this case.'

'I made Sarah's acquaintance when she was with her former owner, and I have long been desirous of purchasing her.'

180

'You know, of course, that she has run away.'

'I do,' he said. 'My offer is made in the event of her return.'

'What makes you think she will return?' I asked. 'She has eluded capture for over a month now.'

He looked down at the knob of his cane, making no reply. After a moment he rubbed at a smudge on the silver with his palm.

'How soon after I accept your offer might I expect her return?' I asked.

Still the infuriating man did not speak. His eyes wandered over the objects on the side table, stopping at the portrait of my father. How Father would have detested him, I thought, and seen through his despicable game. He wanted a wife lighter than he was, but no free quadroon would have him. In spite of his fortune, which I didn't doubt was considerable, he was a laborer. Sarah was perfect for him. They could raise a houseful of yellow brats, one more useless than the next. But what, I wondered, would he do with the baby Sarah already had?

'You know that Sarah has a child with her,' I said.

He looked up from the portrait, his expression candid and businesslike. 'I do,' he said.

'I assume that your offer would include that child. It is too young to be separated from its mother.'

'Of course,' he said.

'You have figured that into the offer, have you?' I said.

He frowned at my persistence on this point. 'I have,' he said.

'Did you know that Sarah has another child?' I asked,

watching his face closely. His eyes widened almost imperceptibly. She didn't tell him, I thought.

'No,' he said. 'I didn't.'

'A boy,' I said. 'A healthy child. She left him behind.' I stood up and pulled the cord for Rose. 'He is eight years old.' Rose came in at the dining room door. 'Send Walter to me,' I said. She looked past me at Mr Roget, then turned back hurriedly. She and Delphine were probably huddled together over the kitchen table in a fit of jabbering. I turned, smiling, to my guest, who had not moved, though his shoulders drooped. The interview was not going exactly as he had planned. 'Walter is old enough to be separated from his mother,' I observed, 'but that is a policy I have always abhorred. It is a cruelty to sell a child away from his only protector. My father, that is his portrait' – I lifted my chin indicating the picture – 'was strongly opposed to the unnecessary breakup of family connections among our people, and I have tried to follow his example.'

Mr Roget listened to these sentiments absently, his eyes focused on the dining room door. I kept my back to it, as I knew exactly what he was about to discover and I felt a great curiosity to see his face when he experienced what I imagined would be a series of hard shocks to the foundations of his scheme. We listened to the patter of bare feet as the wild creature charged across the dining room. Then with what amusement I heard the gleeful bark with which Walter is wont to greet new faces! His hand brushed against my skirt as he hurried past me to clutch the knees of the astounded Mr Roget. I pressed my lips together to keep from laughing. 'It was too bad of Sarah not to tell you about Walter,' I said solemnly. 'I expect she feared you might be disappointed in some way.' Walter was working up to a scream as he attempted to divest Mr Roget of his walking stick. 'You can't have it,' Mr Roget said. 'You might hurt yourself with it.'

'He can't hear you,' I pointed out helpfully. 'He is deaf. He has been examined by a physician, and I'm afraid there is no hope that he will ever be normal.'

Walter gave up the stick and held out his arms to be picked up. When Mr Roget did not respond, he turned to me, stretching his arms up and mewing. He persists in this behavior, though I never touch him if I can avoid it. He was wearing only a slip made from sacking, his face was smeared with what looked like dried egg yolk, his hands and feet were filthy, and his hair was a mass of knots. I looked back to see Rose watching from the far door. 'Come take him,' I said, and she came in quickly. As soon as he saw her, the boy ran to her arms. He was carried back to the courtyard, simpering and patting Rose's cheek. 'He is much improved since our move here,' I observed to Mr Roget as I resumed my seat. My guest raised his hand and commenced rubbing the corner of his eye with his finger, evidently thunderstruck. 'But the truth is,' I continued, 'as you can see, he will never be worth anything to anyone.'

'No,' he agreed. He left off rubbing his eye and gave me a look of frank ill will mixed with grudging admiration, such as one gives a worthy opponent. This gratified me, but his lips betrayed the faintest trace of a smile, an habitual insolence, I thought, which made me want to slap him.

'Perhaps you wish to reconsider your offer,' I suggested.

'No,' he said. 'But as you say yourself, this boy has no value. If I were to agree to take him, I would not offer more.'

'Well, I am curious to hear the figure you have in mind.'

'Two thousand dollars,' he said coolly.

It was twice what Sarah was worth. I allowed the notion of making such a profit and getting rid of Walter in the bargain to tempt me for a moment. I've no doubt I gave Mr Roget the same adversarial scrutiny he had just given me. 'It is a generous offer,' I said. 'You must be very determined to have her.'

'I am,' he said.

What possessed the man? He had already gone to the expense of financing Sarah's escape. He was probably paying someone to hide her as we sat there. If I agreed, he would have to pay to bring her back, then take on two children not his own, one ugly and dark, the other no better than a mad yellow dog. Then he would have to go through the long, expensive process of manumission, applying bribes all round, as the laws are strict. He leaned back in his chair, bringing his stick to the side and stretching his legs out before him, nonchalantly examining his trouser leg. He found a bit of plaster stuck to the seam and flicked it away with his fingernail. It fell onto the carpet near his shoe. I focused my eyes and my mind upon this small fleck of white plaster. The fact of it enraged me, but I counseled myself to remain calm. Mr Roget was waiting for my answer, having no idea that a bit of plaster had sealed his fate and Sarah's as well.

'I fear you are improvident,' I said. 'And that you will regret your offer.'

'That will be my lookout,' he said. 'My offer is firm. I am prepared to write you a check for half the amount today.'

'Let me propose a counteroffer,' I said. 'I think it might prove a more practical solution for us all.'

He glanced at the mantel clock, reminding me that he was a busy man.

'I have no intention of selling Sarah,' I said. 'It's that simple. She is not for sale. However, I would have no objection to a marriage between you. I think that is your object, is it not? She would continue to live here during the week, but she could come to you on Sundays and she would be free to visit one or two evenings a week when I am dining out.'

'You aren't serious,' he said flatly, leaving me to imagine the extent of his outrage. A free man married to a slave! His children would be mine, to do with as I pleased.

'I'm afraid that's all I can offer you,' I said. 'In the event of Sarah's capture, of course, which I firmly believe can only be a matter of days.'

'Then we have nothing more to discuss,' he said, leaning forward upon his cane.

'There are laws against harboring a fugitive, Mr Roget,' I said, 'as I'm sure you know. Assisting Sarah in any way is strictly unlawful. The fines are heavy. Once she has been returned to me, it is my intention to prosecute anyone who can be proved to have aided her in her flight. I don't think of her as having run away, you see, I think of her as having been stolen. She would never take such a risk had she not been encouraged by someone who has no respect for the law, who is so morally derelict that he fails to comprehend the difference between purchase and blackmail.'

Mr Roget stood up, frowning mightily. As I spoke, he drew his head back, as if to dodge the thrust of my argument. 'It is a mystery to me,' I continued, 'how you could find the nerve to come here and offer to pay me for what you have stolen. You seem to think I care for nothing but money. I am going to considerable expense to recover what is mine, by right and by law, and recover her I will.'

'Good day, Mrs Gaudet,' he said, making for the door. I got up from the chair to watch him go. There was the usual bite of pain in my shoulder as my arm stretched down at my side. I didn't expect him to stop, but he did, turning in the doorway to deliver an interesting bit of information. 'You will never find her,' he said. 'She is no longer your property nor anyone else's, and you will never see her again.'

~

'It almost sounds as if he means she's dead,' my uncle said. 'Or else in Canada.' He was stuffing papers into a leather portmanteau.

My aunt picked at a knot in her embroidery. 'Or England,' she suggested.

'Where is Mr Leggett?' I asked.

'He should be in New York by now. His last report was

surprisingly confident. He had what he called "a solid lead." I won't tell you how long it took me to figure out the spelling of that one.'

'So he thinks she has not left the country,' I said.

'I think not,' my uncle said. 'And I trust Leggett on matters of this kind. Roget's remark may well have been braggadocio. He meant that she would leave the country if you refused his offer. But it could take him weeks to arrange a passage for her.'

'He wouldn't send her out of the country and then make his offer,' my aunt agreed. 'What would be the point?'

'Two thousand dollars,' my uncle observed, not for the first time. 'Walter included.'

'I was sorely tempted,' I said.

'How could you accept?' my aunt said. 'He was holding you up for ransom.'

'Not exactly,' my uncle said. 'But it would set a dangerous precedent.' He closed the case and addressed a demibow to my aunt and me. 'Ladies,' he said. 'I must leave you.'

My aunt followed him to the door, then rang for the maid. 'Will you have something?' she said. 'Some cake and coffee?'

'Just coffee,' I said, touching my waist. 'Delphine's cooking is making me fat. She says she can't cook for one person.'

'It's best to give little dinners twice a week and live off what is left for the other days.'

'I don't seem to know anyone anymore,' I said.

'Well, you are in mourning. It's to be expected that you don't circulate. But when you come out, I'm sure you will receive invitations to various parties, and then you will have obligations to your hosts.'

'You are always optimistic,' I said. 'You're more like Father than Mother.'

'Your mother had trials to bear,' she said. 'As you have.'

The coffee arrived. I thought over this remark as my aunt poured out a cup and passed it to me. Was I like Mother? And then it struck me that I had actually turned into my mother. My husband was dead, I lived in her house, I was getting fat, and my hope for the future was that soon I would be giving little dinners for people who pitied me. 'At least she had the memory of a happy marriage,' I said. 'I don't even have that.'

'No marriage is perfect,' my aunt said. 'Your parents' was no more so than any other.'

I thought of Father's diary, of the 'failing' he confessed to, which was so important to Mother that she had kept the record of it until she died. 'Mother was not easy to please,' I said.

My aunt sipped her coffee. She didn't like to hear me speak against Mother. 'She was very gay when she was young,' she said. '"High-spirited" our father used to say, until she made up her mind to marry your father, and then Father called her "mule-headed." She was madly in love with him, enough to make the best of it when she had to go live in a shabby little house with no neighbors but Irish and American upstarts. When you were born, she was overjoyed; you were so like him, so blond and healthy. You were a beautiful child. Even my father came round and invited you all to stay at Christmas. After the two baby boys came, one right after the other, and your father was actually turning a profit on the farm and adding to the house, your mother felt vindicated in her choice. She had two or three happy years. Then the boys both died within days of each other. You probably don't remember that; it was a terrible epidemic. You were barely six.'

'I remember the funeral,' I said. 'At least, I remember that it rained and Father wept.'

'He was devastated, of course,' my aunt said. 'What father would not be? But he allowed his grief to affect his reason.'

This puzzled me, as I remembered my father as the most rational of men. 'In what way?' I asked.

My aunt took another morsel of cake and chewed it thoughtfully. When she had swallowed, she dabbed her lips with the napkin, her eyes fixed upon me solicitously. 'He became obsessed with the negroes. Your mother said it was because he'd not grown up with any. He wrote treatise after treatise on the management of the negro, and he tried to have them published. The *Planter* did take one, but it was by way of a joke, to elicit letters, which your uncle said was quite successful; they got a bundle. He was always talking about what was wrong with the big plantations and how if his system were applied it would be heaven on earth. And of course he was always being disappointed when his own people ran away, or got drunk and sassed him, or pretended to be sick, or fought among themselves. Then he'd make some adjustment to his system, which was basically the same one we all use, the carrot and the stick, but he thought . . . well, it's hard to say what he thought. He seemed to think somehow he was going to make the negroes believe he was God and his farm was Eden, and they'd all be happy and grateful, which, you know, they never are. I remember one night he was going on about the negroes and your uncle became so impatient with him he said, "Percy, they didn't have negroes in Paradise. That's why it was Paradise. They didn't need them."' My aunt laughed at this recollection, which I didn't find particularly amusing.

'All the planters are obsessed with the negroes,' I said. 'Unless they're like Joel and don't think about them at all.'

'That may be,' my aunt agreed. 'But your mother came to feel your father cared more about the negroes than he did about his family.'

I shrugged. 'Father was always attentive to her,' I said.

My aunt studied me a moment, perplexed by my indifference. 'There was something more,' she said hesitantly, though I knew she had every intention of telling me.

'Yes?' I said.

'I think it may be best if you know,' she said. 'It will help you to understand your mother.'

'Then tell me,' I said.

'Your father decided to have no more children,' she said.

I considered this statement. It struck me as rather more sensible than not. As I made no response, my aunt offered a revision to assist my understanding.

'It might be better to say that he lost all desire for more children.'

'He couldn't bear to lose them,' I offered in his defense.

'Yes, that was his reasoning, or so he said. But your

mother was still a young woman. She wanted children, as what woman does not, but more than that, she wanted her husband. He was loving, kind, dutiful, affectionate to her in every way, but no matter how she pleaded –' my aunt paused here, searching for a delicate way to describe an ugly scene and allowing me a moment to imagine my mother's entreaties – 'in their marriage bed, he turned away.'

I sipped my coffee, thinking over this revelation. If this was Father's 'failing,' for which he could not be forgiven, it didn't seem so momentous to me, especially in comparison to my own marriage. I felt perfectly dry-eyed at the thought of Mother weeping to her sister because her husband turned away from her in bed.

'It seems to me it might have been as much her fault as his,' I said.

My aunt gave me a sad look. 'If you had children of your own, you might understand,' she said.

I've heard this before and it never fails to irritate me, but all I said was, 'I don't think so.'

'It has left you with a cold heart,' my aunt insisted.

This stung me. 'If I'd had a husband who didn't outrage all decency every day of his life,' I said, 'I might feel sympathy for a wife who cannot content herself with an upright man.'

My aunt fairly gasped at this retort, allowing the piece of cake she was about to lift to her lips to slip back onto the plate. She cast a nervous sidelong glance, as if someone had just stood up behind her chair. 'We mustn't speak ill of the dead,' she said.

The next morning Joel sent flowers with a card requesting a visit in the afternoon. My conversation with my aunt had left me in a prickly state. I had slept poorly, eaten almost nothing, and my head ached. It was so warm I had Rose open the windows, close the shutters, and sweep out the grate. The room had a bare, unlived-in air that suited me. I knew Joel would tell me of his engagement, relying on my courtesy to spare him any sensation of discomfort. I was not in the mood to be gracious. My patience is at an end, I thought, as Delphine slouched through the room to answer the bell. 'Stand up straight!' I snapped. She jumped as if she had been struck.

Joel came in smiling, dropping his hat familiarly on the desk and turning to me with his hands open, as if presenting an excellent gift. His coat was a new one, fashionably cut, and he gave off a pleasant scent of cologne, pomade, and fresh linen. My appearance was evidently sobering. His smile vanished, replaced by an expression of exaggerated concern. 'But you are still unwell,' he said. 'Your aunt told me your indisposition was only passing.'

'I am well enough,' I said. 'This is just how I look now.'

'No,' he protested, sitting beside me on the settee. 'You are too pale.'

'I don't sleep,' I said.

'Have you consulted a physician?'

'I have sleeping drops,' I said. 'But I don't like to take them because they make me feel dead. Unfortunately, not sleeping has much the same effect.'

Joel looked about the room, noting, I thought, the absence of refreshments on offer. It was too gloomy for him; I was not a gay hostess. What was he to do? 'Perhaps you would like to stroll to the Café des Artistes? A glass of champagne might revive you.'

I smiled. 'I don't think so.'

'Very well,' he said. He sat back farther on the seat and folded his hands in his lap like a boy bracing for unpleasant medicine. He wanted to get it over with, go back outside and play. I decided to release him from his torment.

'Aunt Lelia has told me of your engagement to Miss McKenzie,' I said. 'Please accept my congratulations.'

'I thought she might have.' He sighed. 'I fear your aunt doesn't approve of my choice.'

'She'll relent,' I assured him. 'Just move to the Carré, and raise your children in the Church.'

He chuckled, turning to me. 'Alice has already begun her instruction with Père François.'

Alice, I thought. Alice Borden. It sounded like a steamboat. 'So you are determined to stay in town,' I said.

'Oh, yes.' He gave me a meaningful look. 'There is much to keep me here.'

What, I asked myself, was the meaning of the meaningful look? Neither of us was under the illusion that my opinions had the slightest influence upon him. It would certainly never occur to Joel to include me in the circle who knew about his adventures at the Blue Ribbon Balls, or the likelihood that he would acquire a little house on the Ramparts where he could retire of an evening to be pampered by some poor, trussed-up yellow girl who was ignorant enough to think she was free. No, the meaningful look was simply for show, a courtesy to a poor, crippled widow who must find some way to live on such looks. I am sick to death of this charade, I thought, but I said, 'I'm glad. I should miss your visits.'

'Then you do forgive me,' he said earnestly.

'There is nothing to forgive,' I said.

This reply suited him so well he rushed out ahead of it like a horse scenting the barn. 'I plan to buy a large house, the biggest I can find, and give a series of dinners and dances. As I've explained to Alice, I owe everyone in town. We will have to bring in the wine on flatboats.'

'That will be very gay,' I said.

'It will be,' he agreed. He grasped my hand as if to guide me into a happy future we would share together. 'It will be such a relief to have money,' he said. 'I am mortally sick of being in debt.'

I was uncomfortably conscious of my hand pressed between Joel's. As he spoke, he rubbed the back of my wrist with one finger. It was my bad arm. I could lift my fingers, but I couldn't withdraw it without bringing my other hand in to help. I had not the slightest interest in entering Joel's fantasy about his delightful future. Already the name 'Alice' was tedious to me. I pasted an imbecilic smile on my face while Joel rambled on, but I was thinking gloomily that my aunt was right, my heart was cold.

Yet she was wrong as well, for it wasn't childlessness that had chilled it. It was the lie at the center of everything, the great lie we all supported, tended, and worshiped as if our lives depended upon it, as if, should one person ever speak honestly, the world would crack open and send us all tumbling into a flaming pit. My future was as dark and small as Joel's was bright and wide, yet it was my duty to pretend I did not know it. Was there a man of fortune so disagreeable to other young women that he could be forced to settle for me? And if such a miracle did occur, as my poor aunt deluded herself it might, wouldn't it be understood that I must remain silent, as Alice McKenzie certainly would, while my husband sought solace for my inadequacies in the bed of some light-skinned quadroon? The only woman I knew who had not had to tolerate her husband's fascination with these creatures, which they bred for their own pleasure, was my mother, and now it had been revealed to me that this was because my father was somehow deficient in the urge to procreate. He had refused to bring more children, black, white, or yellow, into this hell where they must suck in lies with their mother's milk.

But it wasn't their mother's milk, I corrected myself. Perhaps that was how the poison entered us all, for even the quadroons were too vain to suckle their own children and passed their babies on to a servant. I recalled watching Celeste nursing my brother at one breast, her own dark child at the other, while my mother looked on approvingly.

Never, I thought. Not me. Let Alice McKenzie have a houseful of Joel's screaming babies; better her than me. I would hold fast to my independence as a man clings to a life raft in a hurricane. It was all that saved me from drowning in a sea of lies.

At length Joel came to the end of his rhapsody and began

to fear that he was tiring me. He released my hand and rose to leave. 'You must take care of yourself, Manon,' he said, looking about the room disconsolately. 'Don't shut yourself up here in the dark.'

'I won't,' I said. I got up to escort him to the door.

'I want you to be well again. I want to see you dancing at my wedding.'

The thought of whirling about in the embrace of some elderly gentleman while my arm hung like a dead animal at my side actually did make me laugh. 'No, no,' I said. 'I'm afraid my dancing days are finished.'

When at last he was gone, I collapsed on the settee, thoroughly exhausted. Mother would never have sent a young man off with so little fuss, I thought, but I didn't care. My eyes rested on the portrait of Father, which is always such a comfort to me, but oddly it had no more effect than the likeness of some stranger in a shopwindow. Father was right; the artist had romanticized him. His jaw was not that strong, his eyes that clear.

I thought of his journal, those banal entries about cotton and weather and disease, and no mention of me, as if I didn't exist, or he wished I didn't, the obligatory mention of Mother as 'my dear wife,' only in connection to his 'failing,' for which he nobly accepted blame.

No, I thought. His failing wasn't his refusal to perform his marital duties and engender more children for the general slaughter, though that was doubtless a symptom. It was something else, something Mother knew but never told, something he had always with him, and took with him, something behind his smile and his false cheer, and the

196

charade of feelings he clearly didn't have. He pretended to be a loving father, a devoted husband, but he wasn't really with us, our love was not what he required, he did not long for us as we longed for him.

He was an impostor.

He kissed me good-night the night he died just as he had a thousand times before; nothing set it apart from any other night when I might find him in the morning, nodding at Mother over the coffee urn. He knew I would never see him again, yet he didn't bother to leave me with so much as an extra word of encouragement, a lingering in the kiss, an extended moment of tenderness, anything that I might have clung to as evidence that he regretted abandoning me, that I figured in his life more importantly than his hoe or a sick field hand, which, after all, received a mention in his journal.

My aunt was right, he was obsessed by the negroes, he wanted them to admire him, to adore him, and my mother was right as well; they had killed him.

I could see myself, so passionate, so terrified, weeping like a fool and calling out to him in the cold wind on the dock. And then I turned to find those boys – did I really see them? – who appeared from nowhere to tell me what no one in my world ever would, the plain unvarnished truth. 'Your pappy started that fire hisself. He shot hisself.'

It was the truth. They had no reason to make up such a story. They were just children, repeating what they had heard. Mother knew it, and it destroyed what was left of her life.

I reached out and laid the portrait facedown on the table.

'Hypocrite,' I said. My head was bursting. It felt as if an iron collar, such as I have seen used to discipline field women, were fastened about my skull. I remembered watching my husband through the spyglass as he stalked across the lawn with one of these devices dangling from his hand. He was in a fury because he'd caught a new girl in bed with the overseer. He passed Sarah, who was feeding chickens in the yard, and spoke to her. I couldn't hear what he said, but judging by the scowl she gave him, it was something insulting. What was it?

'*You're next.*' I heard his voice clearly as I sat there in the darkened room clutching my head. He's dead, I told myself. He's not coming back. But it was as if he were there, leaning over me, turning the screw of the hot iron collar tighter and tighter until my skull must crack from the pressure.

~

It turned cold that night. I was so tired I slept well in spite of it. In the morning, while I huddled over my coffee, Rose and Delphine went about closing the windows and piling coal into the grates. My headache was gone. I felt better than I had in weeks. Let me just live quietly, without illusions, I thought.

When the fire was lit, I took my cup into the parlor and sat at the desk. I could hear the women struggling with the window in Mother's bedroom. It has stuck for as long as I can remember. My thoughts wandered and my eyes traveled over the familiar furnishings until they settled upon a sight I will never become accustomed to: Walter was leaning in the doorway, rubbing his eyes with his knuckles. 'What are you doing here?' I said, as if he had it in him to give me an answer. He dropped his hands, ran across the floor, and threw himself down on the fireplace tiles, letting out a groan of pleasure at the warmth. Before I could call Rose, he turned upon his side and fell asleep.

He's like a cat, I thought, always seeking comfort or making trouble, immune to all commands. Someone had washed him recently and cut his hair in short ringlets. In the firelight it glowed like hot copper wire. His lips were moist and red. I seldom looked at him, but I was in such an idle frame of mind that I noticed his face had grown longer in the last months. Though he had his father's light eyes, he had begun to favor his mother.

Where was she? Philadelphia? New York? Great cold cities full of foreigners. How much longer would it take for Mr Leggett to find her? And at what cost?

Rose came in, looking from Walter to me and back again. 'I thought he was in the kitchen,' she said. 'He snuck out while we was closing up. He always want to be where you are.'

This was true, I thought. He was fascinated by me. 'Leave him,' I said. 'Tell Delphine to fix me a big breakfast. All I ate yesterday was a morsel of bread and a plum.'

∽

Winter settled upon us. The cold seeped around the windows, rose up through the floorboards, even the carpets were cold beneath my thin slippers. I spent the mornings in the parlor, wrapped in shawls, the afternoons at my aunt's, where the fireplace was large enough to accommodate small logs, and the nights shivering beneath a pile of blankets. Walter turned the morning nap by the fire into a ritual. To the amazement of Rose and Delphine, I allowed it. He was there, sound asleep, when my aunt arrived with the news that Sarah had been apprehended at last.

'A gentleman named Foster came to us last night,' she said, breathlessly pulling off her gloves. 'He said he had promised Mr Leggett to relay certain information to us, as he would arrive before the mails. Good heavens, is that Walter?'

'I let him sleep there once,' I said, 'and now he wants to do it every day. Rose says he always wants to be where I am.'

My aunt contemplated the boy, who lay curled on his side, his head resting on his arm. 'What harm can it do?' she said. 'He has certainly grown.'

'He looks like his mother,' I said. 'Where is she.'

'She is in jail in Savannah.'

'But I thought she was in New York?'

'She was. But Mr Leggett has brought her to Savannah. That is where he met Mr Foster and gave him a full account of his travels over dinner at the inn where they both passed the night. It is an amazing story.' My aunt threw off her cloak and composed herself on the settee. 'Come and sit with me and I will tell you all I know. Really, I think Mr Leggett has done himself proud.'

Mr Foster told my aunt that Sarah had boarded the

sailing vessel the *United States* barely a week after my husband's murder, disguised as a white gentleman, Mr Maître, and accompanied by a servant girl named Midge who pretended Sarah's baby was her own. Mr Maître wore dark glasses and hardly spoke, claiming the illness for which he sought treatment in the North made conversation too taxing. He stayed in his cabin, but Midge was all over the vessel, talking to anyone who would listen. Her subject was her poor master and the nature of his illness, which changed from day to day. The captain thought the girl excitable and ignorant. He told Mr Leggett he wondered that a gentleman as frail and distinguished as Mr Maître would tolerate such a giddy piece of baggage, with a screaming baby in tow.

'Distinguished?' I said.

'It seems Sarah makes a presentable gentleman,' my aunt responded. 'Everyone Mr Leggett interviewed remarked on his aristocratic manner.'

Mr Maître disembarked at Savannah and stayed at a boardinghouse for a few days, waiting for a packet ship that would take him on to Philadelphia. Again he kept to his room and his servant fatigued everyone in the place with descriptions of her master's illness. One day it was his eyes, the next his heart. The baby screamed unceasingly; the landlady believed it was colicky. She too wondered how the gentleman put up with his companions. When they left, the whole house breathed a sigh of relief.

Mr Maître boarded the *Atlantic Clipper* as soon as it docked, but the winds were unfavorable and the ship sat at anchor for three days. The captain took an interest in his passenger, who was, he thought, sick unto death. He had the cook prepare thin gruel, which was the only thing the gentleman said he could hold down. Often he encouraged Mr Maître to go up on deck to take the fresh air, but he was unsuccessful.

When they reached Philadelphia, though Mr Maître had booked his passage through to New York, the captain urged him to spend the night onshore while the ship discharged its cargo. He recommended a rooming house nearby. The captain told Mr Leggett that he feared his passenger would not last the night. When he came on deck and saw the lights of the town, Mr Maître was so weak he clung to the rail and wept.

He survived the night, and in the morning they set sail for New York. The winds were favorable, the trip without event. Mr Maître began to eat, his servant ran out of auditors, and the baby stopped crying. When they arrived in New York, Mr Maître expressed his gratitude to the captain; he told him he had saved his life, and went down the gangway with a steady step. He was met by a gentleman and a lady, who evidently expected him. They entered a cab and drove away.

A good bit of Mr Leggett's time and energy went to interviewing the cabdrivers who picked up fares at the dock that day. Eventually he was directed to a house in Brooklyn belonging to a Mr and Mrs Palmer. When he learned from the neighbors that the Palmers were Quakers, he knew he had found his quarry.

'What are Quakers?' I asked.

'Some sort of religious society,' my aunt explained,

'much opposed to slaveholding of any kind, I gather.'

Mr Maître had abandoned his disguise at the Palmers' and become Miss Claudia Palmer, a cousin of the family visiting from the South. Mr Leggett began a constant surveillance of the house. A few days later Mr Palmer went out in a cab with the servant Midge and the baby. He came back alone. Mr Leggett didn't see either of them again. The next day Mr Palmer was observed on the docks, inquiring into the availability of passage to England; the next he was at the customs office filling out forms. For several days, nothing happened. Miss Palmer rarely left the house, except to take brief walks with her cousins. Mr Leggett despaired of capturing her in their company. Any public scene might result in Sarah's arrest. The free negroes and others like these Quakers were known to protest police actions with such vehemence that the writs could not be served and the prisoner was released. Mr Leggett watched for his opportunity and hired two strong men to be at the ready when the time came.

Again Mr Palmer was observed on the docks, and this time he purchased a single berth in the name of Claudia Palmer, on the *Commodore*, bound for London. Mr Leggett knew his chance had come, and that it would be his last.

He called his men, hired a closed carriage, and arrived at the crowded wharf early on the morning of the ship's sailing. There these three were met by an actress, paid and coached in advance. When Sarah arrived, accompanied only by Mr Palmer, Mr Leggett was sure of success. He had one of his men begin to abuse the actress just as the couple approached the gangway. He relied upon Mr

Palmer's religious principles to distract him, and he was right. Mr Palmer turned away from his charge and attempted to interpose himself into the quarrel. Immediately the couple turned upon him, beating him cruelly. There were cries for help, all eyes were riveted on the violent scene. Mr Leggett and his other man came up on either side of Sarah and grasped her by her arms. 'It's time to go home, Miss Sarah,' Mr Leggett said. She cried out to Mr Palmer, who was unable even to hear her through the noise and confusion. Mr Leggett and his man led her quickly to the carriage, shoved her inside, and drove away.

'You are right,' I said, when my aunt had finished. 'It is a remarkable story. What I wonder is what it will all cost. I suppose I will have to pay for the actress and the strong men.'

'Your uncle thinks Mr Leggett acted properly. It is cheaper to pay an actress than bribe a bailiff.'

'I suppose so,' I said.

'Mr Leggett is waiting in Savannah for three other runaways who are being transported from a jail in South Carolina. Then he and a trader who has six more slaves to bring to market here will drive them all on foot overland very cheaply.'

'That will take weeks,' I complained.

'Yes,' she said. 'It will be a long walk for Mr Maître.'

I sniffed. 'What a name.'

'Your uncle cautions you that Sarah may be very different when she returns,' my aunt said. 'She has passed as a free woman, and that experience is generally deleterious to a negro's character.'

'She has done more than that,' I observed. 'She has tasted a freedom you and I will never know.'

My aunt looked perplexed. 'What is that?' she said.

'She has traveled about the country as a free white man.'

~

Whatever Mr Leggett saved by sending Sarah overland was swiftly paid out to Dr Landry, for she arrived more dead than alive. They had cropped her hair close somewhere along the way, and with her sunken eyes and cheeks, her bony limbs, she looked like a skeleton. She had a racking cough that kept the whole house awake all night. In the trek through the swamp she had contracted some manner of foot rot, which smelled as bad as it looked. When Dr Landry's treatments proved ineffectual, my aunt suggested sending for Peek, who arrived straightway with her poultices and infusions. She set an iron pot boiling in the courtyard which sent a stench over the whole neighborhood. She put Sarah on a cot in the kitchen with the fire going and kettles boiling day and night until it was like a steam bath and Delphine nearly fainted from the heat. Dr Landry disapproved, but he advised that sometimes negroes could only be cured by other negroes, which proved correct. I didn't burden him with the information that all her life my mother had followed every palliative he offered with a dose of something Peek had mixed up. Gradually Sarah began to eat, the cough abated, even her feet dried out and crusted over.

Mr Leggett's bill was two hundred and fifty dollars,

205

which I thought outrageous. He had itemized it completely, down to the actress's cab fare and the charge for shackles at the jail in Savannah. He and my uncle determined to find a way to convict Mr Roget of abetting Sarah's escape. Mr Leggett wanted that reward as well, and my uncle had his own reasons.

They had no luck trying to trace the tickets, but it didn't take them long to learn that Mr Roget had commissioned a slave-catcher named Pitt to bring in the talkative Midge, so notorious on the Eastern Seaboard for her intense interest in the health of Mr Maître. It seemed Midge had found the North so much to her liking that she refused to return to her master. 'We will trap him through his own arrogance,' my uncle declared. Mr Leggett departed to collect sworn testimonies.

As for Sarah's baby, no one seemed to know what had become of it. When I asked Sarah, she coughed a few times and said, with her usual forthcomingness, 'She dead.'

My uncle was wrong; Sarah was not much changed. She was as sullen as ever. As her health improved and she was able to work again, she performed her tasks without comment or interest, but she was more competent than most, certainly better than Rose, who had a more pleasing manner. No one could dress my hair so well as Sarah, nor care for my clothes, nor arrange the rooms. She continued to evidence an aversion to Walter.

One morning, as she was serving my breakfast, Walter came in and commenced pawing her skirt and whining to be picked up and petted, as Rose was always so willing to do. Sarah put down the coffee urn, laid the flat of her hand across his face, and pushed him away roughly. He ran bawling from the room.

'Does he remind you of someone?' I said, earning one of her thinly veiled looks of contempt. She took up the urn and leaned over me to fill my cup.

'He's as much your responsibility as mine,' I said. 'God knows, I didn't ask for him, but here he is.' She went to the sideboard and stood with her back to me, slicing a baguette, indifferent as the knife in her hand.

'It's useless to talk about responsibility to you people,' I continued. 'You have no sense of it. That's the gift we give you all. You just run away and we bring you back and you never have the slightest twinge of conscience. No one ever holds you responsible for your actions. It's just assumed you have no moral sense.'

She spooned a dab of Creole cheese next to the bread and brought it to me. I placed my right hand on the plate to hold the bread, then took up the knife to spread the cheese. 'It's thanks to you I'm a cripple,' I said. 'Look at the way I have to eat.' She stood to the side, watching my hands with an interested expression.

'If you hadn't beat me to the horse,' I said.

It was the first time I'd spoken to her of that night, though I dreamed of it often enough. I was running, running, and the horse was there, if I could only get to it, but someone was holding me back. Sometimes it was my husband, sometimes Sarah, sometimes a man I didn't know. Once I turned to find Mother clawing at me, her teeth bared like a wild animal. I woke from these dreams soaked in perspiration, my heart racing so fast it hurt.

Sarah stood watching me, her hands folded at her waist. She was listening to me, I thought, which gave me an odd sensation.

'You knew my husband was dead,' I said. 'There was no reason for you to run. They weren't going to kill *you*.' I took a bite of bread and glared at her as I chewed it. She met my gaze, but curiously, as if she wondered what I would say next.

'But you had already hatched your plan with Mr Roget, hadn't you?' I said. 'I heard you whispering here that night. You had it all arranged; your clever disguise, and your ship passage, and your new friends in the North. I'm sure they all made you feel very important, very much the poor helpless victim, and no one asked how you got away or whom you left behind.'

Her eyes wandered away from me, to the plate on the table, the cup next to my hand. A strange inward-looking smile, as at a recollection, compressed her lips. 'When you gets to the North,' she said, 'they invites you to the dining room, and they asks you to sit at the table. Then they offers you a cup of tea, and they asks, "Does you want cream and sugar?"'

I was dumbfounded. It was more than I had ever heard her say. My uncle was right, I thought. She had changed; she'd gone mad. I took a swallow of my coffee. 'And this appealed to you?' I asked.

'Yes,' she said, raising her eyes very coolly to mine. 'It appeal to me.'

I considered this image of Sarah. She was dressed in borrowed clothes, sitting stiffly at a bare wooden table while a colorless Yankee woman, her thin hair pulled into a tight bun, served her tea in a china cup. The righteous husband fetched a cushion to make their guest more comfortable. It struck me as perfectly ridiculous. What on earth did they think they were doing?

This one thing we wish to be understood and remembered, – that the Constitution of this State, has made Tom, Dick, and Harry, *property* – it has made Polly, Nancy, and Molly, *property*; and be that property an evil, a curse, or what not, we intend to hold it.

—Letter from A. B. C. of Halifax City to the *Richmond Whig*, January 28, 1832

Acknowledgments

Those familiar with the Library of America's compilation *Slave Narratives* will recognize in my character Sarah's journey north an indebtedness to the intrepid William and Ellen Craft. Disguised as a sick white man and his slave (Ellen taking the master's role), the Crafts bought two train tickets and escaped from bondage in Georgia, 'running a thousand miles for freedom.' The Crafts' account was widely known in the nineteenth century, and Professor Henry Louis Gates has speculated that 'Hannah Crafts,' the escaped slave who penned a recently discovered novel, may have chosen her pseudonym as an homage to Ellen Craft.

Other books that informed my vision of the master/slave relationship in the antebellum South are Herbert Apetheker's *American Negro Slave Revolts*, Liliane Crete's *Daily Life in Louisiana, 1815–1830*, John Hope Franklin and Loren Schweninger's *Runaway Slaves*, Mary Gehman's *The Free People of Color of New Orleans*, Walter Johnson's *Soul by Soul: Life Inside the Antebellum Slave Market*,

Harriet Martineau's *Society in America*, Alton V. Moody's *Slavery on Louisiana Sugar Plantations*, Joe Gray Taylor's *Negro Slavery in Louisiana*, and Christine Vela's *Intimate Enemies*. The journals of two Louisiana plantation owners, Rachel O'Connor and Bennet H. Barrow, were eminently useful.

Thanks to Dr Philip Castille for his comments and conversation. For their continuing encouragement and support, I am indebted to Nikki Smith, Nan Talese, John Cullen, and Adrienne Martin.

To Margaret Atwood, whose help far exceeded the expectations of an already invaluable friendship, this novel is affectionately dedicated.